Falling for the Rodeo Cowboy

Widowmaker's head crashed into the wooden slats directly below Alyssa. The impact sent her flying.

For a brief, surreal moment, she was a bird, a kite, a piece of confetti. The world spun around her, a kaleidoscope of blue sky, cheering faces, and grandstand. Then she hit the ground inside the arena with a bone-jarring thud.

Alyssa tried to stand, but her limbs wouldn't cooperate. She was like a marionette with its strings cut.

A shadow fell over her. Two strong arms hauled her upright. She blinked, heart pounding, and focused on the face in front of her. *Riley Manchester. Of course.*

"What in the world were you thinking?" he growled.

It was a good question. Alyssa wished she had an answer.

FALLING FOR THE
Rodeo Cowboy

JoAnn Charles

Prairieland Press

Prairieland Press
PO Box 2404
Fremont, NE 68026-2404
Printed in the U.S.A.

Cover Design by Prairieland Press
Book Design by Prairieland Press

eBook ISBN-13: 978-1-944132-55-2
Paperback ISBN-13: 978-1-944132-54-5
Hardcover ISBN-13: 978-1-944132-53-8

Prairieland Press

For Larry, who always supports my dreams,
and for Mom and Dad, Always!

One

ALYSSA

ALYSSA PRESSED her cheek against the window, eager for any distraction from the endless plains that had marked the last hours of the bus ride. It had been years since she'd last traveled by bus—college, maybe—long enough that she'd forgotten how it made her back ache and her thoughts wander.

But as the hayfields of green and gold gave way to brick streets and vintage storefronts, she blinked in disbelief. Her mother's description of "picturesque" hadn't quite captured it.

Bluestem looked like a town from one of those 1960s movies. Not quite real. For a moment, she wondered if she'd stepped through a doorway and landed somewhere else, maybe in another time altogether.

She reached for the diamond ring that now hung around her neck. She twisted it between thumb and forefinger, the habit half-comfort, half-reminder of everything she'd lost. Could three months in a place like this really help her escape the pain of the past three years?

The bus hissed to a stop in front of a weathered brick hotel with a painted sign announcing, "The Whitemore." Alyssa shouldered her camera bag, wrestled her suitcase from the overhead compartment, and stepped down onto the sidewalk. Children darted around a wrought-iron patio set in the hotel's garden, their laughter ringing out—a sound that tugged at her heart, a bittersweet echo of the family she and Trevor had once dreamed about.

"Lyss!"

Alyssa turned to see her godmother, Maggie, standing at the hotel's entrance, waving enthusiastically.

Relief flooded through her. Maggie hadn't changed a bit, still graceful and poised with that distinctive streak of silver in her elegant chignon. If Alyssa didn't know better, she would swear that Maggie had lived her life as a dancer, rather than the editor and owner of a small Nebraska newspaper.

Alyssa offered a tired wave as she navigated the uneven path toward her godmother.

Maggie enveloped her in a hug, gentle but fierce. "It's so good to see you, sweetheart. How was the trip?"

"Long," Alyssa said, though just being here, seeing Maggie, made her feel more alive than she had in months. Maybe her mother was right. Maybe time away from Chicago was just what she needed.

"One suitcase? That's all you brought?" Maggie asked, arching a brow.

Alyssa grinned. "Of course not! Mom and Dad are shipping the rest by UPS."

"Ah, that explains it." Maggie grabbed the suitcase handle. "You look exhausted. Let's get you inside and settled."

Maggie led Alyssa through the front doors, the ivy-framed archway of the old hotel welcoming them inside. Alyssa paused in the doorway. The lobby featured high tin ceilings with ornate crown molding, antique furniture that looked genuinely period rather than reproductions, and a grand staircase that wound its way to the upper floors.

"This place is amazing," Alyssa said, pulling her camera out of its bag. "Do you think they'd mind if I took some pictures?"

"Of course not," Maggie said, a smile tugging at her lips. "If anything, LeAnne will be flattered."

Alyssa circled the lobby, snapping photos from every angle. Photography had always been her escape, long before it became her job. Through the lens, she could control what she saw, how she saw it. The world made more sense, framed and focused. "It's incredible. Like stepping into the past."

"That's the idea," Maggie said. "The Whitemore has been here since the early 1900s. At first, it was built for railroad passengers, but no train's come through Bluestem in years. Now it's mostly tourists. History buffs, or folks traveling the Outlaw and Cowboy Trails."

A colorful poster behind the front desk caught Alyssa's eye: Bluestem Annual Rodeo. The bold text popped against a backdrop of rodeo clowns, bucking broncos, and barrel-racing cowgirls.

"Is the rodeo really this weekend?" Alyssa leaned in for a closer look. "I've never been to one."

"Then this is your lucky day!" Maggie said, her tone suspiciously cheerful.

Alyssa narrowed her eyes. "Why?"

"Because that's your first assignment for the paper. To cover the rodeo and get us some shots for the weekend edition."

Alyssa turned, eyebrows raised. "My first assignment? I just got off the bus. Don't I get a day to settle in?"

"The rodeo's not until this weekend, so you have plenty of time," Maggie said. "But I want our readers to see it through fresh eyes—your eyes."

"I don't know anything about rodeos."

"I know. That's what makes it perfect. You'll capture what it feels like to experience it for the first time."

Alyssa sighed. She'd worked with enough editors to know that arguing would be pointless. And wasn't this why she'd come? To work, to focus on something other than her grief, to rediscover her passion for storytelling?

Maggie sensed Alyssa's hesitation. She

leaned in, lowering her voice as if sharing a secret. "Besides, what better way to start your summer than with a bang? Or, maybe in your case... a buck."

Alyssa let out a groan, but her smile gave her away. "That's an awful pun, Maggie. Just awful."

Maggie squeezed her arm. "Exactly! That's why I need you working for the paper. My jokes —and my headlines—get cheesier by the day."

Before Alyssa could respond, movement from a doorway behind the desk drew her attention. A young woman emerged, her warm smile directed at them both. Dressed in a cotton blouse and paisley skirt, her long auburn hair pulled back with a matching headband, she looked like she'd stepped out of the mid-twentieth century herself.

"You must be Alyssa." The woman extended her hand. "I'm LeAnne Hudson, the innkeeper here at the Whitemore. I'm so pleased to have you staying here this summer."

"Thank you for having me," Alyssa said. "This hotel is absolutely stunning."

"It's been in our family for generations," LeAnne said, her pride clearly showing in her voice. "My siblings and I are the third generation of Hudsons to own it. We've kept as much of the original character as possible, but the Wi-Fi's solid and every bed's got memory foam. Best of both worlds."

Maggie checked her watch. "Is it that time already? I need to get back to the Gazette. Lenny's waiting for my final approval on today's layout." She turned to Alyssa. "LeAnne will take excellent care of you. Get some rest, and I'll pick you up at six. We'll eat dinner at my place. How does that sound?"

"Perfect," Alyssa said, fighting a small, irrational pang of abandonment. *I'm here to work for Maggie, not to be coddled by her*, she reminded herself.

Maggie gave her one more quick hug before heading out, the door chiming softly behind her.

"Let me show you to your room," LeAnne said, plucking a key from a wooden board behind the desk. Each hook had a small brass plaque below it with a name. "All our guest rooms are on the second floor."

She gestured toward the staircase Alyssa had been photographing earlier. Up close, it was even more striking—wide wooden steps that curved gently upward, with intricately carved banisters polished to a warm glow by decades of hands sliding along them.

"Here, let me take that for you," LeAnne said, reaching for Alyssa's suitcase.

"I can manage," Alyssa said, but LeAnne was already lifting it.

"It's part of the service. Besides, these steps can be tricky in heels if you're hauling luggage."

Alyssa glanced down at her stilettos and conceded the point. "Lead the way, then."

As they climbed, Alyssa ran her fingers along the banister, feeling the subtle imperfections that spoke of age and use. The staircase opened onto a wide hallway lined with doors, each with its own brass nameplate.

"Your room's at the end of the hall," LeAnne said, guiding her past doors labeled Johnny Carson and Fred Astaire. "Each room honors a famous Nebraskan. Some guests are familiar with their person. Others learn something new during their stay."

They stopped at a door with a plaque reading Bess Streeter Aldrich. LeAnne handed over the old-fashioned key.

"Aldrich was a novelist who wrote about pioneer life in Nebraska. She had this amazing way of making small-town life feel universal. Maggie thought you'd appreciate staying in a room named for a fellow storyteller."

Alyssa swung the door open, revealing a charming room that felt both historically accurate and comfortably modern. A queen-size bed dominated one wall, covered with a handmade quilt in shades of blue and cream. Sunlight filtered through lace curtains and fell across a writing desk beneath the window.

"Your bathroom's through there." LeAnne pointed to a door on the right. "And this—" she opened another door "—leads to your sitting room."

The sitting room was small but inviting: an armchair, a compact sofa, and a bookshelf crammed with old books, including several by Aldrich. A second window overlooked Main Street.

Alyssa peeked out. From here, she could see the colorful awnings of shops, people strolling the sidewalks, and, in the distance, the spire of what must be a church.

"I'm a long way from Chicago," she said softly.

LeAnne laughed. "I've never been to Chicago.

But I've been to Nashville a few times. All that traffic. And the noise! I never get a good night's sleep when I'm there."

Alyssa shrugged. "You get used to it. The city has its own rhythm." She paused, thinking of her apartment's view of a neighboring brick wall and the constant hum of traffic. Had she ever really noticed Chicago's rhythm, or had she just learned to tune it out?

LeAnne straightened a small wildflower bouquet on the side table. "I'll let you get settled. But once you're ready, I'd love to treat you to lunch at Daisy's Diner. Best way to get to know Bluestem is to meet folks over a good meal."

Alyssa longed for nothing more than a hot shower and a nap, but her rumbling stomach refused to be ignored. Besides, she was here to work, and that meant getting to know the town. "I'd like that," she said, stifling a yawn. "Thanks."

"Wonderful!" LeAnne said, her eyes brightening. "I'll meet you in the lobby in fifteen minutes. Fair warning, though—you're going to be the talk of the town for at least a week. New faces are big news around here."

After LeAnne left, Alyssa sat on the edge of

the bed and ran her hand over the quilt. Silence filled the room: no sirens, no neighbors' music, no elevator machinery. Only the occasional creak of the old building and the distant sound of a car passing on Main Street.

She pulled out her phone and sent a text to her parents. "Arrived safely. My room is lovely. Going to lunch with the innkeeper. Will call tonight."

Then she stood and moved to the window, looking out at the town that would be her home for the next three months. The brick streets, the vintage storefronts, the unhurried pace of people walking by—it was all so different from what she'd known.

Her fingers found the ring at her neck again, and she closed her eyes. *I'm here, Trevor. I'm trying.*

When she opened them, the view hadn't changed, but something inside her had shifted just slightly. Maybe, just maybe, this place could offer her what Chicago no longer could: a chance to breathe, to heal, to find her way back to the person she used to be.

Two

ALYSSA

FIFTEEN MINUTES LATER, Alyssa descended the grand staircase to find LeAnne waiting, her auburn hair now pulled back in a neat ponytail.

"Ready for your first taste of Bluestem?"

Alyssa nodded, grateful for LeAnne's easy warmth. "Absolutely."

"It's just a couple blocks. Let's walk."

Alyssa welcomed the chance to stretch her legs and take in the new scenery. The afternoon sun warmed her shoulders as they strolled down Main Street, past storefronts with hand-painted signs and window boxes overflowing with petunias.

"Mrs. Mendelson!" LeAnne called out to a

silver-haired woman kneeling in a flower garden. "Your roses are gorgeous this year."

"Thank you, dear! I'm trying that new fertilizer Sawyer Jennings recommended." Mrs. Mendelson looked up, shading her eyes. "And who's this?"

"This is Alyssa Downing, Maggie's new writer at the Gazette."

"Welcome to Bluestem, dear. Looks like you're headed for lunch at Daisy's."

"Guilty as charged," LeAnne said with a laugh. "First stop for any new Bluestem resident."

Mrs. Mendelson nodded approvingly. "Smart choice. Try the blueberry pie if she hasn't already sold out."

A few doors down, a man with rolled-up sleeves was sweeping the sidewalk outside a brick building with "Boesart Hardware" painted across the window.

"Alyssa, this is Mr. Boesart. He runs the hardware store. Mr. Boesart, this is Alyssa Downing."

Mr. Boesart leaned on his broom, his weathered face creasing into a smile. "From Chicago, right? Maggie said you'd be coming today. My nephew went there for college. Said the pizza was good, but the people walk too fast."

Alyssa laughed. "That's probably true. I'm looking forward to a slower pace."

"Well, you found the right place for that." He gestured down the street with his broom. "If you need anything—paint, light bulbs, advice on fixing a leaky faucet—you know where to find me."

They rounded the corner and stopped in front of a sunny yellow building, its patio bustling with people enjoying lunch beneath a striped awning. A chalkboard sign welcomed visitors to Daisy's.

As they approached, a few heads turned their way. The lively chatter lowered to a murmur, and Alyssa caught sight of a woman at a nearby table leaning over to whisper to her companion.

Heat crept into Alyssa's cheeks. In Chicago, she would have blended into the crowd; here, she was clearly the main headline. She'd wanted a fresh start, but maybe not quite this fresh.

LeAnne ducked inside to request a table, leaving Alyssa to wait on the patio. She pulled out her phone, grateful for something to do with her hands. Through the lens, Bluestem looked like something from a postcard: a vintage Chevy parked at the curb, kids on bikes racing past, a toddler giggling as he shared his sandwich with a patient golden retriever. The kind of scene that would make her Chicago friends roll their eyes—but it made something in her chest loosen.

"Smile, Bluestem," Alyssa whispered, backing up for a better angle. Her heel caught on a crack in the sidewalk. She stumbled, grabbing the edge of a nearby table for balance. It jostled just enough to send a cup of coffee toppling over a stack of papers.

Three startled faces—two men and a woman—looked up at her.

"Sorry! I'm—I'm so sorry!" Alyssa stammered, trying to regain her balance and her composure.

"Great. Just great." The sandy-haired man closest to her scowled at the spilled coffee and soaked paperwork. "Dad wanted this paperwork an hour ago. Now we'll need to start all over again!"

Alyssa's stomach dropped. Of course. She couldn't even make it through her first hour in town without drawing unnecessary attention to herself.

"Riley, it's fine," the woman at the table said, her tone gently chiding before she offered Alyssa a kind smile. "Ignore my brother. There's nothing here that can't be redone. No harm done at all."

Alyssa grabbed napkins from the dispenser and tried to mop up the mess, painfully aware of Riley's glare burning into her. Her fingers trembled as she dabbed at the wet pages. "I really am sorry. I can pay for reprinting, or—"

"Give me those," he said gruffly, reaching for the napkins. Their fingers brushed, and an unexpected spark shot through her hand.

Alyssa pulled back in surprise, nearly dropping the napkins altogether. *What was that?*

His brown eyes met hers, and for a heartbeat, his irritation flickered into something else—confusion, maybe, or surprise. Then the scowl returned, and he looked away, jaw tight.

"There you are!" LeAnne said, weaving through the tables. "I see you've bumped into the Manchesters!" She gave Alyssa a quick, encouraging smile, before turning back to the trio. "Riley, Kate, Carter. I'd like you to meet my newest guest, all the way from Chicago. She's working for Maggie at the Gazette this summer."

The man called Carter grinned, his eyes crinkling with amusement. "Making quite a splash already, I see."

Alyssa felt heat creep up her neck. She managed a weak smile. "I promise I'm not usually this clumsy. Or this destructive."

"Could've fooled me," Riley muttered, still dabbing at the papers.

Kate shot him a look before turning back to Alyssa. "Welcome to Bluestem. Don't let Riley scare you off—he's not usually this rude."

Riley frowned, but his shoulders relaxed slightly. "Sorry. It's just been one of those days."

Before Alyssa could stammer out another apology, a cheerful voice called from indoors: "LeAnne, your table's ready!"

LeAnne waved in response, then smiled at the trio. "So great to see you all. Enjoy the rest of your lunch."

Alyssa followed LeAnne to the door, but paused at the threshold to glance back at the Manchester table. Kate had turned her attention back to the damp papers, but the two men were still watching her.

Carter gave a friendly nod and a wave, while Riley's gaze lingered, unreadable, as he absently rubbed his fingers together. Their eyes met briefly, and Alyssa felt that same inexplicable tingle she'd experienced when their fingers touched.

She turned away quickly, her heart doing an odd little flutter.

LeAnne and Alyssa slid into a booth, the vinyl squeaking beneath them. A small vase with a single daisy adorned the table, its cheerful white petals a stark contrast to the lingering embarrassment Alyssa felt.

LeAnne's eyes sparkled with barely suppressed amusement. "Well, you certainly know how to make an entrance. It's not every day someone disrupts a meeting of the Manchester trio."

Alyssa groaned and covered her face with her hands. "I can't believe I did that. I wanted to disappear into the crowd—only there was no crowd!"

"Don't worry. It'll only be the talk of the town for about a week, then something better will come along."

Alyssa's eyes widened in horror.

LeAnne laughed. "I'm teasing. Trust me, by tomorrow, everyone, including the Manchesters, will have forgotten all about it." She paused, her smile turning knowing. "Though I noticed Riley couldn't seem to stop looking at you."

"He was glaring at me," Alyssa corrected, dropping her hands. "There's a difference."

"Mm-hmm." LeAnne's tone suggested she wasn't convinced. "Now, let's order. I'm starving, and you need comfort food after that introduction."

Alyssa picked up the menu, but her mind kept drifting back to brown eyes and that unexpected spark when their hands touched.

She shook her head. The last thing she needed was to complicate her life right now. Even if that spark had felt like something she hadn't experienced in a very long time.

Three

RILEY

RILEY WATCHED ALYSSA WALK AWAY, trying not to notice the apologetic smile she cast over her shoulder. He forced his attention back to the soaked documents that lay ruined on the table. The coffee had transformed the neat text into an illegible blur.

Riley sighed, glancing at his watch—he was forty minutes late as it was. His phone buzzed on the tabletop. *Chute's ready. Bulls are restless. You comin'?*

He drummed his fingers against the table, the lingering warmth from Alyssa's brief touch forgotten beneath the pressure of another commitment slipping away. Between keeping his dad happy with his work at Manchester

Trucking and keeping himself sharp for the rodeo, Riley was always running behind.

"So ..." Carter said, a sly grin creeping onto his face. "What do you think of LeAnne's guest?"

Riley glanced up from the ruined paperwork. "Who? Alyssa? I think she's clumsy."

Kate laughed. "Clumsy, sure. But cute, right?"

"I didn't notice," Riley said. He sounded grumpy, even to himself. "I was too busy trying to save our morning's work."

"Right," Carter said, laughing. "You were practically drooling. Never thought I'd see this day. My little brother going all gooey-eyed over some city girl."

"Gooey-eyed?" Riley asked. "You need your own eyes examined."

Carter chuckled. "You're not fooling anyone, little brother. I saw the way you looked at her. The same way you looked at Shelby, before she dumped you for that doctor."

"Don't try to deny it," Kate said, teasing. "Even I saw the sparks flying."

Riley rolled his eyes. His siblings had an annoying habit of seeing right through him. "I have no idea what you're talking about. And for the record, I was the one who ended things with Shelby. Caught her looking at that doctor's BMW like it was made of gold. Told her she could have him, his medical degree, and his BMW. I've got better things to do than be someone's second-best option."

He glanced toward the door where Alyssa had disappeared, those impractical stilettos clicking against the tile, that overpriced leather handbag swinging from her elbow—just like Shelby and her endless parade of things he could never afford.

"Speaking of sparks," he said, pointing his fork at his sister, "how's it going with you and that lawyer, Kate?"

Kate shrugged. "All business, no sparks. Just the way I like it."

Carter made a face. "Sounds real exciting."

Kate narrowed her eyes at their older brother. "We're taking it slow." She leaned back, arms folded, stubborn. "Not everyone rushes into things."

"Rushing in can be fun," Carter said. "At least I know what I want."

"Really?" Kate's voice dripped with sarcasm. "And what exactly do you want, dear brother.

First it was Dani, then Sarah, then—who was it last month? Jessica?"

While Kate and Carter continued to spar with each other, Riley grabbed the check and headed inside. He spotted Alyssa in a booth with LeAnne, laughing. The sight made his heart skip a beat.

He turned away, cursing under his breath. What was he thinking? His life was already a juggling act—training for the rodeo, handling his responsibilities at Manchester Trucking, and navigating their father's expectations and goals.

Adding a woman, especially a woman like that, into the mix was the last thing he needed. Alyssa was just passing through, and once she left, he'd be right back where he was after Shelby left—alone and wondering what the point had been.

Four

ALYSSA

ALYSSA NUDGED her way through the crowd, her camera tucked securely by her side. The Bluestem Rodeo was in full swing—the air rich with the scent of dust, leather, and sweet kettle corn. She'd already filled a memory card with safe, ordinary shots from the sidelines: kids eating cotton candy, parents fanning themselves in the stands, a cowboy tipping his hat to a fan.

"Excuse me," she said as she weaved past a family sharing a funnel cake. The bull-riding event was in full swing. This was exactly the shot she needed to make her article come alive for her readers.

Through the slats of the fence, Alyssa

watched a hulk of a man get bucked off after three seconds. *Pathetic*, she thought, and she wasn't thinking about the ride. Her vantage point was useless. Every shot ended up with the rails slicing across it, like she was camped out at the local jail, not at the rodeo.

She scanned the perimeter until she spotted a cowboy stationed near the gate—a leathery old man with a weathered face and a stern expression. Alyssa approached him with her most professional smile.

"I'm covering this for the Bluestem Gazette," she said. "Can I step a little closer to the chute for a better angle?"

The man shook his head. "Sorry, ma'am. No one gets past this point without clearance from the stock boss."

"Is he around?"

He pointed across the arena to a man in a dusty hat. "He'll be tied up 'til after the bull riding's done."

Alyssa tried again. "What about the press area?"

He jerked his chin toward a small roped-off section in front of the stands. "Right there."

She headed in the direction he pointed. Four photographers crowded the so-called press area, standing shoulder to shoulder. She tried to squeeze in, but it was hopeless.

A voice crackled over the loudspeakers. "Next up, Riley Manchester on Widowmaker."

Alyssa's head jerked up. Riley? The businessman from the diner? It couldn't be. She stood on her tip-toes, trying to see around the men in front of her, but it was useless. She had to get a better look.

Her eyes drifted to the fence. Weathered wood, sun-bleached and scarred. Before she could talk herself out of it—before the rational part of her brain could remind her this was reckless and unprofessional—she slung her camera across her back and grabbed hold of the wooden rails.

"Brilliant idea, wearing shorts," she muttered, wincing as splinters bit into her thighs. At the top, she wobbled and grabbed hold of a post to steady herself. The view was perfect. She could see the whole arena, the crowd, even the dusty parking lot that framed the rodeo grounds. She raised her camera and adjusted the zoom, focusing on the chute.

A horn blared. The crowd roared as the gate burst open. A massive black bull exploded into the arena. The rider on top clung to the bull's back with a tenacity that seemed to defy common sense, his body snapping like a whip with each violent jerk and twist.

Alyssa raised her camera and clicked off a rapid series of shots, capturing the raw power of the bull and the precarious balance of the rider. Sweat trickled down her forehead, and she wiped it away with the back of her hand, never taking her eyes off the scene below.

As the rider shifted his weight to counter the bull's savage twists, his face came into view. Alyssa's pulse quickened. She immediately recognized the tousled sandy hair beneath the helmet. It was the same guy! She couldn't believe it!

He moved with the bull's wild bucking as if he were an extension of the creature. As the bull twisted and turned, Alyssa's lens followed. The first few seconds were chaos. Then, like a gift, the scene crystallized. The man's confident grin and the bull's threatening horns, perfectly framed against the blue sky. Alyssa's finger clicked the shutter, and she almost whooped with joy. She'd gotten the shot, the one she'd been waiting for.

The horn sounded again, signaling the end of the ride. Riley bailed and hit the ground running, sprinting for the fence as the bull wheeled around, nostrils flaring. Alyssa held her breath, her finger still on the shutter, capturing every frame of Riley's escape. He vaulted over the barrier just as the bull's horns grazed his boot.

The rodeo clowns moved in, distracting Widowmaker with their gaudy costumes and fearless taunting. The crowd erupted. Alyssa exhaled, a smile spreading across her face.

She checked the display on her camera. Each shot was a gem, a perfect sequence of a near-tragic dismount. Relieved, she lowered her camera. She was done. She could go back to the Gazette now and start writing.

"Nice ride, Manchester!" someone shouted, and Alyssa watched Riley wave in acknowledgement.

Then the bull turned. Alyssa's smile vanished as the animal charged toward her section of the fence. Widowmaker's head crashed into the wooden slats directly below her. The impact sent her flying.

For a brief, surreal moment, she was a bird, a kite, a piece of confetti. The world spun around her, a kaleidoscope of blue sky, cheering faces, and grandstand. She heard screams and the shrill whistle of a clown's toy horn. Then she hit the ground inside the arena with a bone-jarring thud.

Alyssa lay still, dazed, her body a collection of dull aches and sharp pains. The roar of the crowd and the heavy thud of the bull's hooves on the arena floor filtered through her haze. She tried to process what had just happened, her mind a blur of fear and adrenaline.

Alyssa tried to stand, but her limbs wouldn't cooperate. She was like a marionette with its strings cut.

A shadow fell over her. Two strong arms hauled her upright. The world tilted. She blinked, heart pounding, and focused on the face in front of her. *Riley Manchester. Of course.*

"What in the world were you thinking?" he growled, half-dragging her toward the front gate of the arena while the rodeo clowns worked to distract the angry bull and drive him toward the exit chute.

It was a good question. Alyssa wished she had an answer.

She tried to speak, but no words came. She was used to the sympathy of friends; to the gentle understanding of people who knew about Trevor and the strain she'd been under these past three years. Riley's attitude was something entirely different.

When the pair were safely out of danger, Riley's grip loosened. Her legs gave out and she crumpled to the ground.

Riley stood over her, hands on hips, totally oblivious to the small crowd gathering around them. "Now, tell me. Just what were you doing on top of that fence?" he asked.

"I ... wanted a closer shot," she said. She hated how thin her voice sounded.

"A closer shot? A closer shot?" His voice rose. "This isn't some fashion shoot, City Girl. These bulls can kill you."

The harsh edge in his voice stung. Alyssa knew she should be apologetic, maybe even grateful for his daring rescue, but the sting of his words ignited something in her, a spark of defiance fueled by the grief that was always a part of her.

She wiped her hands on her shorts, smearing the dirt into streaks. "It's my job."

"Your job is to climb fences and topple into arenas?" he asked, eyebrows raised in disbelief.

She glared at him. "My job is to be a journalist."

He frowned at her. "Some journalist you are."

Alyssa's temper flared. Who did this guy think he was? "Sorry. I didn't realize riding bulls made you an expert on journalism. You want to give me some tips?"

He didn't miss a beat. "Here's one: Don't get yourself killed. Makes for a lousy story."

Riley's jaw clenched, and for a moment, Alyssa saw a flicker of something besides anger in his eyes. Was it worry? Admiration? But as quickly as it appeared, it was gone.

"Get yourself checked out at the medics' tent," he said. Without waiting for her response, he turned and walked away, disappearing into the crowd of riders clapping him on the back and shaking their heads at the close call.

Alyssa looked down at her camera, her throat tightening. The memory card was probably fine, but the camera itself was ruined. The screen cracked; the body dented. Trevor had given her this camera four years ago for her birthday, the last birthday they'd spent together. Another piece of him gone.

She blinked hard, refusing to cry in front of strangers. She brushed at her clothes, dislodging clumps of dirt, acutely aware of how out of place she must look—a city girl in over her head.

Alyssa took the outstretched hands of the couple of remaining folks and steadied herself on her feet. They offered to take her to the medics' tent, but she waved them off with a tired smile. Turning away, she trudged toward the parking lot and Maggie's car. She needed a shower, a change of clothes, and a good cry.

As she passed the food stands, she heard snippets of conversation. People were talking about the girl who tumbled into the arena during the bull ride, guessing at her identity and motives. Great, she thought. More fuel for the Bluestem gossip mill.

Alyssa slumped into the driver's seat, head pressed to the steering wheel. The afternoon's events replayed in her mind: the adrenaline, the terror, Riley's voice, sharp and angry. Her camera lay beside her in the passenger seat. She reached over and touched it gently, as if it were a wounded animal.

She'd come to Bluestem for peace and healing, but she was starting to wonder if she was like this camera—battered and broken beyond repair.

Five

RILEY

THE SUN BEAT down on Riley as he gripped the hammer, sweat trickling down his back and soaking his shirt. It had been two days since Alyssa's cartwheel into the arena, but the image still haunted him, sour and raw, every time he replayed it in his mind.

"She had no business climbing that fence," he said, driving a nail into the weathered wood with more force than necessary.

Carter steadied the fence post, his movements unhurried and deliberate. "She was just doing her job, Riley."

"Without a helmet. In shorts!" Riley's jaw clenched. "It was just plain stupid."

Carter laughed. "Probably," he said. "But

everyone walks away with a bruise or two from the rodeo. You know that better than most."

Riley grunted, refusing to dignify that comment with a response. He couldn't shake the image of Alyssa, sprawled like a rag doll in the dirt, that camera still clutched in her hands. He wasn't sure he would ever forget that moment.

"Seriously, Ry. Why are you getting so worked up about this?" Carter pulled on the newly fixed post, testing its sturdiness. "I don't remember you being this concerned when Emily Thompson fell barrel-racing last year. And she broke her shoulder in two places!"

Riley hesitated, the hammer heavy in his hand. "That was different," he said, not meeting Carter's eyes. "Emily's a pro. Alyssa was just careless."

Carter shrugged. "Maybe. But you've got to admit, scaling that fence took guts." He paused and shot Riley a sly grin. "And Kate's right. She is pretty darn cute. Maybe that's what's got you so riled up."

"You think everyone's cute," Riley said, setting the new post in its hole.

Carter laughed. "What can I say? I have an eye for beauty."

Riley rolled his eyes. "Whatever. I still say she's reckless."

"Or passionate. You know something about that, don't you?"

Riley didn't answer. Instead, he swung the hammer again, the sound of metal on wood echoing across the open field. He worked with a fierce intensity, as if each strike could knock his thoughts into order.

Carter's voice broke through Riley's musings. "You know, it's okay to admit you like her."

Riley's hammer stilled mid-swing. He turned to face his brother, brow furrowed. "I don't... I mean, she's not..."

"Not what?" Carter asked, a knowing grin spreading across his face. "Not the most interesting thing to happen in Bluestem since they put in the slide at the swimming pool?"

Despite himself, Riley felt a smile tugging at his lips. "Aw, c'mon now. That slide's got nothing on her." The words slipped out before he could stop them, and he felt a flush creep up the back of his neck.

"Ha! I knew it. Just ask her out already!"

Riley frowned. "Why would I do that?"

"Because if you don't, I will. And because it's

better than stewing about Dad's offer and your future."

Riley knew his face betrayed him, the corners of his mouth lifting despite his best attempt at a scowl. "Just drop it, okay?"

Carter held up his hands. "Fine. No more talk about Alyssa. For now." He stretched, casting a long shadow over the grass. "So let's talk about you. And your future."

A knot tightened in Riley's gut. "Which part?"

Carter's voice lost its teasing edge. "The part where Dad expects you to take over as CEO of Manchester Trucking. The part about choosing between the rodeo or sitting behind a desk."

Riley stared at the post, tapping the nail lightly, then harder, each strike more deliberate than the last. "I'll finish the season and see how I feel."

Carter crossed his arms, his stance more confrontational than usual. "Riley, you can't keep putting this off. Dad needs to know where you stand."

Riley's hammering stopped. "I just don't see why I have to choose. Plenty of guys do both. Rodeo on weekends, work during the week."

"It's not just about balance, Riley. It's about what you really want."

Riley glanced at Carter, taking in the dust on his jeans, the sunburn peeling on his arms. After their mother died, Carter had selflessly stepped in and taken over the day-to-day workings of the ranch so their father could focus all his energy on their trucking business.

"It was simple for you," Riley said. "You always knew what you wanted. Bluestem. The ranch. You never had to choose."

Carter laughed, a short, bark-like sound. "Simple? Oh, little brother, if only you knew."

The sun climbed higher, and Riley could feel the heat baking the sweat that coated his arms.

"Just talk to him," Carter said. "That's all I'm saying."

Riley fell silent, knowing Carter was right but not ready to admit it. They worked without talking, the only sounds the clink of tools and the rustle of the grass. Their father was a man of few words but strong opinions, and Riley feared that voicing his true feelings would open a rift between them that, unlike this fence, he could never mend.

Six

ALYSSA

ALYSSA STARED at her computer screen, fingers resting on the keyboard as she reviewed her last paragraph. The soft chatter of her coworkers and the hum of the ancient air conditioner blended into a comforting white noise. She tapped the last period and leaned back in her chair, stretching her arms above her head.

She swiveled to look out the window. Main Street was alive with a familiar cast of characters, and Alyssa loved being its audience of one. The florist across the street was meticulously adjusting her sunflower arrangement, while the barber took his customary smoke break. A group of teenagers claimed their usual spot in front of the library, deep in conversation.

Even after a month, she still found Bluestem as charming as she had that first day when she and LeAnne had walked together to Daisy's Diner.

"Alyssa, honey? Could you come in here for a minute?"

Alyssa saved her document—"Bluestem Beekeeper Buzzes with Joy". There was an undercurrent of something in her godmother's tone that Alyssa couldn't quite place. Hesitancy? Excitement? A bit of urgency?

Alyssa made her way through the cramped office, weaving between file cabinets and stacks of old newspapers, until she reached Maggie's glass-walled office.

"You wanted to see me?" she asked, leaning against the door frame.

Maggie sat behind her cluttered desk, her silver hair secured in its usual neat twist, her reading glasses dangling on their chain. But instead of her usual calm demeanor, she was practically vibrating with excitement; her phone clutched in one hand.

"I did. Come in and close the door, will you?"

Alyssa's stomach knotted. Memories of the last time she'd attended a closed-door meeting flitted unbidden through her mind—the day of Trevor's accident.

"Sit, sit. You have to see this," Maggie said, waving her phone.

Alyssa sank into the chair, her hands clasped tightly in her lap.

Maggie leaned forward, eyes sparkling. "Remember that photo you took at the Bluestem Rodeo? The one of Riley Manchester during the bull riding event?"

Alyssa nodded slowly, her pulse quickening at the mention of that day and her tumble into the arena.

"Well, it went viral." Maggie turned her phone around, showing Alyssa the screen. "Look at this. It's everywhere—Facebook, Instagram, even the State Rodeo Association's official page. Twenty thousand shares and counting."

Alyssa's jaw dropped as she stared at the image. There was the cowboy, suspended in mid-air, his body a perfect arc of controlled power and grace, the bull beneath him a blur of motion. The late afternoon sun had caught them both at the exact right moment, creating an almost ethereal quality to the shot.

"I... I had no idea," Alyssa whispered.

"Neither did I until this morning when the secretary of the State Rodeo Association called." Maggie set down her phone, her expression shifting to something more serious. "They want you, Alyssa. They want the photographer who took this shot to cover the rodeo in Scottsbluff this weekend."

Alyssa blinked, stunned into silence. "They… what? Why? I'm not an expert on rodeos. Or even a competent spectator, apparently."

"Oh, nonsense." Maggie waved her hand dismissively. "You don't know anything about beekeeping, either. But that didn't stop you from writing about it." She rifled through her papers, her silver bracelet jingling, and slid a printout across the desk. It was an email from the rodeo association, its logo prominently displayed at the top.

"But how would I even get there? Borrowing your car to drive around town is one thing, but across the state?"

Maggie laughed. "Already handled. The Association's arranging transportation and lodging."

Alyssa's eyes widened. "They are?"

"They are," Maggie said, her silver chignon

bobbing slightly. "And here's the best part. They want the Gazette to handle distribution to all their members. Think what this could mean for our circulation!"

She paused, her expression growing more somber. "Alyssa, honey, I haven't wanted to worry you, but the paper's been struggling. Ad revenue is down, subscriptions are dropping. This contract could keep us afloat for another year, maybe longer."

The weight of those words settled over Alyssa like a blanket. She'd known the Gazette was small, but she hadn't realized how precarious things were. Maggie had given her a lifeline when she'd needed it most, and now she had a chance to return the favor.

Maggie reached across the desk, squeezing Alyssa's hand. "This could be good for you, Lyss. For both of us, really. The Gazette needs this boost, and you... well, maybe it's time to break out of your cocoon and stretch those wings again."

A flicker of guilt for all she owed Maggie battled with her deep-seated reluctance. Besides, she was out of objections, at least ones she could voice aloud.

"All right," she whispered. "I'll do it."

"What was that?" Maggie cupped her ear, leaning forward.

"I said I'll do it," Alyssa repeated, a small smile tugging at her lips.

"Wonderful!" said Maggie. "Now, let's get back to work, shall we. I need that beekeeping story by three this afternoon."

Back at her desk, Alyssa stared at her screen without seeing the words. Her mind flashed to thoughts of the Bluestem Rodeo and Riley Manchester's angry face as he pulled her from the arena. Would he be at this rodeo, too?

She shook her head, dismissing the thought. He was a businessman. He didn't have time to travel across the state to every rodeo in Nebraska, did he?

Alyssa pulled up the viral photo on her own computer, studying it with fresh eyes. She'd captured something real in that moment, something magical. The way the sunlight caught the dust kicked up by the bull, the determination in Riley's eyes, the pure energy of the moment—it was all there in a single frame.

Maybe Maggie was right. Maybe it was time to stretch her wings again.

She sighed and leaned back. This wasn't just a chance for the Gazette to get noticed or to see more of the state. It was a chance to prove to herself that she could still do this work, that she could still find the extraordinary in the ordinary. And, most importantly, a chance to escape Bluestem and avoid another awkward run-in with Riley Manchester, at least for one weekend.

Seven

ALYSSA

ALYSSA'S DESK at the Gazette looked like a tornado had swept through a rodeo library. Books and magazines covered every inch of surface space, their glossy pages reflecting the afternoon light streaming through the window.

She chewed absently on the end of her pen while flipping through an oversized book about bull riding techniques. The taste of plastic did nothing to soothe her growing anxiety.

She set the book aside and opened her laptop. A woman in a cowboy hat and rhinestone-studded shirt wheeled a horse around a barrel, kicking up dust. Alyssa watched the video in awe as the cowgirl guided her horse around each barrel with stunning precision.

The video ended, and Alyssa closed her laptop with a sigh. She leaned back in her chair, gazing at the ceiling as if it might offer a graceful way to back out of this assignment. Nothing. Just the familiar ridges of the popcorn ceiling and a water stain she swore looked like a cowboy hat. She rubbed her temples, trying to massage away the headache forming behind her eyes.

"Alyssa, I brought you a package." Hannah, the Gazette's receptionist, walked in and handed Alyssa a small box. "I think it's another rodeo book."

"Probably," Alyssa said, though she made no move to open it.

"How's the crash course in Rodeo 101 coming?" Hannah asked.

"Let's just say I won't be joining the circuit anytime soon."

Hannah picked up a book and thumbed through it. "Do you really need to know all this just to take a few photos and write a story?"

Alyssa laughed. "No. Probably not. But I want to be prepared. This is a big deal for Maggie and the Gazette."

Hannah perched on the corner of the desk. "This goes way beyond prepared. It's not like you actually have to ride a bull, you know." She paused, a mischievous glint in her eye. "Though I'd pay good money to see that."

"Hilarious," Alyssa said, but she felt the start of a genuine smile tug at her lips. "You aren't helping, you know."

Hannah laughed. "Sure I am. That's the first time I've seen you smile all week!"

Alyssa watched Hannah walk away, wishing she could borrow even a fraction of her carefree nature. She reopened her laptop and hit play, the sound of galloping hooves and cheering crowds filling the room once more.

Eight

ALYSSA

THE CRUNCH of gravel jolted Alyssa from a restless sleep. She bolted upright, fumbling for her phone. 6:47 AM. *What? How could that be?* She'd meant to be up an hour ago. She shuffled to the window and yanked the curtains aside, squinting against the morning light. An old blue pickup truck idled in the driveway, its exhaust creating small clouds in the cool morning air.

She couldn't see the driver, but the sight of the truck made her stomach twist. She just realized that she'd agreed to ride half-way across Nebraska with some guy she didn't know! What had she been thinking? She never would have agreed to this in Chicago.

Alyssa could almost see Hannah rolling her eyes at her paranoia. "Maggie is the one who arranged for your ride, right? And Maggie would never do anything to hurt you. You know that. So stop looking for excuses and go have a great weekend!"

Alyssa nodded to herself, dressed quickly, and headed down the stairs.

LeAnne stood at the bottom of the stairs, a travel mug of coffee in her hand. She handed the steaming drink to Alyssa. "Looks like your chariot awaits," she said, giving Alyssa's shoulder a gentle squeeze.

Alyssa grimaced, stepped onto the porch, and froze. There, leaning against the dusty truck, was Riley Manchester. In his cowboy hat and jeans, he could have been a model for a western romance novel.

Her stomach did a little flip-flop. Her overnight case slipped from her fingers, landing with a thud on the wooden planks.

"Morning," Riley said, tipping his hat. He pushed off the truck and crossed the yard in long, easy strides before climbing the three wooden steps to the porch landing.

"Mr. Manchester," she said, her voice cracking with surprise. "I thought... I mean, I didn't know...I thought the rodeo committee was sending someone."

"Please. Call me Riley. Mr. Manchester is my dad." Riley rubbed the back of his neck. "And they did send someone. Me. Maggie thought you might appreciate having someone you already know as your escort, and the Association agreed."

She forced a polite smile, trying to ignore the way her heart hammered against her ribs. "That was . . . kind of them."

"Plus, they wanted someone who has experience rescuing you when you tumble into the arena." A small grin tugged at the corner of his mouth.

Alyssa felt her cheeks flush with heat. *Great. He just had to go there, didn't he.* "Don't worry," she said, her tone more defiant than she'd intended. "I plan on staying firmly outside of the arena from now on."

"Good plan," Riley said, nodding.

Alyssa reached for the handle of her overnight case just as Riley's hand closed around it, their fingers making contact for the briefest moment.

He hesitated, his hand remaining on hers for a heartbeat longer than necessary, then gave a gentle, almost apologetic smile. "I've got it," he said, taking the case from her. His eyes shifted to the camera bag slung across her shoulder, and he extended his hand, palm up.

After a moment's hesitation, Alyssa slipped the strap over her head and passed it to him, watching as his fingers curled protectively around the worn leather.

She retreated a step, crossing her arms tightly against her chest—a shield against both the early morning chill and the way her pulse quickened at his nearness.

"Thanks," she murmured, watching as he carefully stowed her gear in the bed of his old Ford. The truck looked to be at least ten years old, with faded blue paint and dents that spoke of hard work and long miles. It suited the cowboy. But she wasn't sure how it fit into the world of the businessman she had met that very first day at Daisy's Diner.

Riley shut the truck bed with a soft clang and

walked back to where Alyssa stood, waiting. "Ready?" he asked, opening the passenger door for her.

"As ready as I'll ever be," she said, and climbed into the cab of the truck.

Nine

RILEY

RILEY SLID into the driver's seat. He stole a glance at Alyssa, who was white-knuckling her purse in one hand while struggling with her seat belt.

"Controls are here—seat warmer, lumbar support, air conditioner." He tapped the console panel with its row of cryptic symbols.

She gave a quick nod, not meeting his eyes. The silence stretched between them, filling the truck cab like an unwelcome third passenger.

He had known this was a bad idea the minute the president of the Association had called him. But how could he say "no"? The president had already promised Maggie they'd handle Alyssa's transportation to and from the rodeo. Since Riley was the only cowboy from the area traveling to Scottsbluff this weekend, it just made sense that he was her escort.

He couldn't help wondering if Maggie had orchestrated this whole situation when she'd called in that favor. No doubt she had. Maggie's sharp mind was unmatched in Bluestem, except perhaps by his own sister Kate.

He cleared his throat. "How are you settling into life here in Bluestem? And at the Gazette?" He kept his eyes on the road, but he could feel her tense up beside him.

"It's ... different," she said, staring out her window. "I'm getting used to it."

Riley nodded, more to himself than to her. "Must be quite the change from what you're used to. Chicago, right?"

"Right," she said, then fell silent again.

"And your work?" he pressed, surprising himself with his own persistence. Something made him keep talking when keeping silent would have been easier. "I've seen some of your stories in the Gazette. They seem... interesting."

Alyssa turned toward him, one eyebrow arched. "Which ones?"

Riley's mind went blank. He tried to picture the article Carter showed him online, something with Alyssa's name attached. "The one about the... bake sale."

Alyssa's hazel eyes narrowed slightly. "You mean the farmer's market?" she asked.

"Right, the farmer's market," Riley said quickly. "And the one about the... uh... drought impacts on local farms? Great information."

Alyssa's lips tightened. "Thanks, but I didn't write it. That was a piece we got from the state's news wire."

Riley winced. "Okay, you got me," he said. "I haven't actually read any of your articles. Except the one about the Bluestem Rodeo. That one I did read and it was good. Really good."

Alyssa's guarded expression softened slightly. "Thanks," she said.

"The dust, the crowd, the energy—it was like being there all over again. You even made me look good." He paused, then couldn't stop himself from adding, "Though it brought back some pretty vivid memories of your own grand entrance that day."

Alyssa let out a small, reluctant laugh. "That was something, wasn't it?"

Riley smiled, genuinely surprised that she could laugh at herself. Something in his chest loosened, like ice cracking during a spring thaw. "You know, not everyone's first rodeo experience is such a dramatic one. You're practically a legend now."

She rolled her eyes but didn't seem resistant to his banter. "A legend for what? Nearly getting trampled by a bull?"

He shrugged. "Walking away from that is achievement enough," he said with a half-smile. "Believe me, I know. And all legends have to start somewhere. Even local legends."

A familiar country tune crackled through the old truck's speakers. Without thinking, Riley joined in, his rich baritone filling the cab. "I was raised on the banks of a river..."

Mid-verse, his voice faltered and died as he suddenly remembered he wasn't alone. He glanced sideways at Alyssa, heat crawling up his neck.

Her eyebrows lifted, clearly surprised. "A business man, a cowboy, and a singer," she said. "What other talents are you hiding under that cowboy hat?"

Riley let out a sheepish laugh. "Sorry," he said. "Force of habit. Especially when one of Dani Whitemore's songs comes on."

"Dani Whitemore? She's originally from around here. Right?"

"You mean LeAnne hasn't told you about her?"

"No. Why would she —" Her eyes widened. "Wait! Is she related to LeAnne?"

"Yep. Dani is LeAnne's big sister, off chasing her dreams in Nashville. She uses their grandmother's maiden name— Whitemore, like the hotel."

"No way! I had no idea!"

Riley nodded, unable to hide his hometown pride. "She's really making a name for herself. Bluestem's claim to fame!"

Alyssa tucked a strand of hair behind her ear, a small smile playing at the corners of her mouth. "Oh, I don't know about that," she said. "With that voice of yours, you could give her some serious competition, if you wanted."

"Me? Not a chance. I much prefer singing in the shower and the truck to singing on stage."

"Well, then, don't let me stop you."

Riley's smile widened as he picked up the melody again, his voice stronger now. Halfway through the chorus, Alyssa's voice slipped in alongside his. Just a whisper at first, then louder. Fuller.

Song after song, their voices intertwined in one makeshift duet after another. Initially harmonious, the tunes gradually took on a more carefree and imperfect quality as the miles ticked by.

As Riley navigated a bend in the road, he shifted his gaze to sneak a quick look at Alyssa. There was a newfound ease in the way she sat. He could see the wall she had built between them crumbling, note by off-key note.

A new song began, and Riley launched into it with gusto. Beside him, Alyssa joined in, but after a few lines, her voice trailed off. The melody continued without her.

Riley glanced over, his brow furrowing slightly. "What's wrong? Don't know this one?"

Alyssa shook her head, forcing a small smile that didn't quite reach her eyes. "No, I do." She paused, her fingers fidgeting with the strap of her purse. "Trevor used to love this song."

The name hung in the air between them—unexpected, weighted with unspoken history.

Before Riley could respond, Alyssa turned away from him toward the window. "Oh, look at that barn," she said, pointing out the window at a weathered red structure in the distance. "The way the paint is peeling—it's kind of beautiful in a rustic way, don't you think?"

Riley let her redirect the conversation, but he filed away that moment, that name. Trevor. Whoever he was, he'd left a mark.

They continued down the highway, and gradually the music worked its magic again. When the last notes of a familiar drinking song faded away, they both erupted into laughter.

"Oh man," Riley chuckled, wiping a tear from his eye. "I haven't butchered a song that badly since tequila night at the Rusty Spur."

Alyssa snorted—a genuine, unguarded sound that made Riley's pulse quicken.

"You should hear me attempt Dolly Parton. It's a crime against music," she said, with mock despair.

Riley shook his head. "I didn't peg you for a country music fan," he said.

Alyssa shrugged and smiled. "There's a lot you don't know about me, Riley Manchester."

The way she said his name sent a little shiver down his spine. "Well," he said, "we've got the whole weekend ahead of us. Maybe we can change that."

Alyssa hesitated, her smile fading slightly as she studied him. Her eyes, warm amber in the morning light, held a wariness that made Riley wish he could take back his words. Maybe he'd been too forward.

"Maybe," she finally said, her voice soft but not cold.

A comfortable silence settled over them—not the tense, awkward quiet from the beginning of the drive, but something warmer. Something that felt almost like friendship.

Riley glanced over at her, a genuine smile softening the lines around his eyes. "You know," he said, deliberately injecting a teasing tone into his voice, "you're not so bad ... for a city girl."

Alyssa turned to look at him, and the change was subtle, but he felt it. She smiled back, her own voice taking on a playful warmth. "You're not so bad yourself, for a country boy."

As if on cue, John Denver's familiar fiddle intro filled the truck cab. "Talk about your perfect timing!" Riley said. He turned the volume dial up, gave Alyssa a playful wink, and joined

Denver in the chorus, loudly proclaiming, "Thank God I'm a Country Boy."

Ten

ALYSSA

RILEY PULLED into the Scottsbluff rodeo grounds just after eleven. Alyssa marveled at the sprawling clusters of pickups, trailers, horses, and people filling every inch of the parking lot. The air smelled of dust and hay, and the announcer's voice crackled over the loud-speaker.

Riley jumped down from the cab and jogged around to Alyssa's side of the truck to open the door for her. The gesture was straight out of another era, and she wasn't sure whether to be charmed or annoyed. Probably both, she decided, as she stepped down from the cab.

His hand lightly touched her forearm. "I

need to register for my event," he said, sounding genuinely apologetic. "You'll be okay on your own?"

"Absolutely. This isn't my first rodeo," she said, with a teasing grin.

Riley laughed. "True enough. How could I forget?" With a wave, he headed off toward the arena, his tall frame easily visible as he weaved his way through the crowd.

Alyssa watched him go, her mind a whirl of conflicting thoughts and emotions. It startled her how much she'd wanted to ask him to stay by her side for just a while longer.

The man was practically a stranger! She thought back to the dread she'd felt when she'd first seen him that morning. She'd braced herself for a journey marked by tense pauses and forced politeness. Instead, their off-key singing and simple conversation had made her forget, just for a little while, the gnawing loneliness she carried with her.

Whatever was happening, she needed to shut it down. Fast. The pain of losing Trevor was still a raw wound. Getting attached to anyone, especially a small-town businessman playing cowboy on the weekends, could only lead to more heartache, and she wasn't ready for that.

She shook her head. *Heartache? Getting attached?* This was ridiculous. They'd shared one ride and four hours of singing along to the radio. That was all. And the moment they'd pulled in, he was gone, busy doing his job. She needed to do hers.

She pulled out Maggie's camera and scanned the area. The lens gave her a comforting sense of distance, a way to observe without participating: kids dressed in cowboy gear, teenagers taking turns on a mechanical bull, old-timers chewing tobacco and surveying the proceedings with practiced eyes.

Alyssa strolled through the rodeo grounds. She snapped a series of photos of cowboys meticulously preparing their gear, their calloused hands working with the familiarity of long practice. The click of her shutter blended with the hum of conversations, the whinnies of tethered horses, and the rustling of canvas awnings.

She wandered toward the stables, where four children took turns gently stroking a colt, under the watchful gazes of both its protective mare and their owner. One little girl shrieked with delight as the colt nuzzled her hand, and Alyssa captured the moment, freezing her wide-eyed wonder in a single frame.

Just outside the stables, she spotted a woman braiding a horse's mane with practiced fingers.

"She's beautiful," Alyssa said.

"She's more than beautiful," the woman said, patting the horse affectionately. "She's a born winner—together we've taken first place in the barrel race the past three years."

Alyssa extended her hand. "I'm Alyssa Downing. I'm writing an article for the rodeo association. Would you mind if I took some photos?"

"Go right ahead," the woman said, standing a little taller.

"Are you racing her again this year?"

The woman shook her head. "I'm getting too old for this. Passing the reins to my daughter." She gestured to a teenage girl standing shyly behind her. "Jenna's got the talent to take her far."

Alyssa turned to Jenna, her expression curious. "Following in your mom's footsteps. Are you excited?"

Jenna nodded, though Alyssa could see a touch of fear.

"I am. I just hope I don't mess up."

"You won't," Alyssa said with an encouraging smile. The words felt familiar, an echo of a conversation she'd had with Maggie just the night before. It was strange hearing her own doubts reflected in Jenna's voice. "I'll be looking forward to your ride." She snapped a couple more photos, then moved on.

Each person she spoke with added another piece to the mosaic she was creating in her mind. A young couple waiting in line for the mechanical bull recounted their first meeting at this very rodeo five years earlier. An aging vendor shared how the rodeo circuit was like a second home to him, and the other vendors his extended family. A boy, no older than eight, bounced on his toes while he waited for his mutton busting debut, his eyes gleaming as he showed off his new helmet covered in dinosaur stickers.

As Alyssa made her way through the maze of

parked trailers, a man leaning on a cane caught her eye. His jacket, decorated with bright rodeo patches, quietly told the story of his past glories.

"That's quite the jacket," Alyssa said. "Were you a competitor?"

The man's laugh rumbled deep in his chest. "Still am, between these ears." He tapped his temple before rubbing his knee with a wince. "A bull decided my leg looked better bent sideways. That was ten years ago next month."

"Do you miss it?" Alyssa asked, already knowing the answer from the look in his eyes.

"Every day," he said, then added with a grin, "But watching these kids try their luck almost makes up for it. Almost."

She thanked him and moved on to a cluster of teenage girls on horseback. They were debating which cowboys were worth their time at the dance that night, using a scale from "forget it" to "hands off—he's mine."

One girl with a long braid showed Alyssa her turquoise belt buckle. "My grandmother wore this during her first barrel race," she said. "She gave it to me for luck two years ago, and I haven't lost a race since."

Everywhere she looked, there was a narrative

waiting to be told, a moment waiting to be captured. This task was a refreshing change from the hurried assignments she'd tackled in Chicago. Here, the stories flowed freely, told with pride and without pretense. People welcomed her questions, eager to share their passion.

She thought back to all the research she had done to prepare for this trip. Each book claimed rodeo was a way of life for those involved. She now truly understood what that meant. The people she talked to weren't just taking part in a weekend hobby; they were pouring their hearts into every competition.

Alyssa made her way to the arena. Children wearing miniature boots and oversized hats chased each other around the stands while they waited for the show to begin. The smell of popcorn and hot dogs wafted from the concession stand and mingled with the scent of dirt and livestock.

She had just climbed to the top of the stands and found a secure spot with a perfect view of the arena when a voice over the loudspeaker invited the crowd to stand for the Grand Entry.

Alyssa watched in awe as riders streamed

into the arena in precise formation, flags snapping above them. Her lens captured a barrage of color: sequined shirts, embroidered vests, fluttering bandanas.

The riders formed a long line, then split into two, creating a corridor down the center of the arena. A lone rider carrying the American flag burst through, the fabric snapping crisply against the sky.

Alyssa lowered her camera, wanting to experience this moment directly. As the national anthem played, she felt a swell of emotion, suddenly aware that she was part of something larger than herself.

When the music ended, Alyssa cheered just as loudly as the lifelong fans around her.

The announcer introduced the saddle bronc event, and just like that, the rodeo was underway. Alyssa watched, transfixed, as the first competitor settled into position.

When the gate burst open, her camera worked frantically, capturing the wild dance between man and horse. She counted seconds with the crowd, holding her breath until the buzzer sounded.

Time seemed to stand still for Alyssa as one event led seamlessly into the next. Between events, she caught glimpses of Riley. He moved through the crowd with ease, stopping to chat with riders, spectators, and officials. Once, their eyes met across the arena. He tipped his hat to her, a small smile playing on his lips. Alyssa felt heat rise in her cheeks and looked away, focusing intently on adjusting her camera settings.

When the announcer called Riley's name, her throat went dry. She raised her camera, her finger hovering over the shutter button.

The gate swung open, and the bull leapt into the arena, twisting with a ferocity that left Alyssa stunned. Riley's body was a study in balance and grit, moving fluidly as he fought to stay on.

One ... two ... three ...

Her camera worked relentlessly, capturing every split second of his struggle: the tense line of his jaw, the blur of the bull's frenzied motion, the tight grip of his hand on the rope.

Four ... five ... six ...

The noise from the stands was deafening as the crowd chanted down the seconds. Alyssa clenched her teeth anxiously, willing him to hold on.

Seven... eight!

The buzzer sounded just as the bull gave a massive buck. Riley flew off, landing hard in the dirt. He rolled quickly, narrowly avoiding the bull's stomping hooves as the rodeo clowns moved in to distract the animal.

The stands erupted. Riley stood, dusted himself off, and waved to acknowledge the applause. His eyes found Alyssa's across the arena. She lowered her camera and gave him a thumbs up.

As he made his way out of the arena, she felt a strange mix of relief and exhilaration. She scrolled through the photos on her camera, marveling at the intensity captured in each frame. Here, amidst the rodeo chaos, Riley's charm was mesmerizing, a stark contrast to the polished professional she'd met that first day at Daisy's.

The rest of the afternoon passed in a blur of events. Alyssa circled the arena, documenting the grace of barrel racers, the precision of team ropers, and the gritty determination of steer wrestlers. Between shots, she collected quotes from winners and consoled the disappointed, always hunting for the human stories behind the spectacle.

As the last event wrapped up, her feet throbbed and her camera felt like it weighed twenty pounds. She made her way to the concession area, lured by the smell of grilled meat and the promise of a cold drink. As she stood in line, a familiar voice called out her name. She turned to see Riley jogging towards her, his hat in his hand and a broad grin on his face.

"Hey there, City Girl," he said as he caught up to her. "How was your second day at a rodeo?"

Alyssa laughed. "Much better than my first. I managed to stay on the right side of the fence the whole time."

"So I noticed." Riley's grin widened. "Listen, a bunch of us are heading to the steakhouse just down the road. Thought you might like to tag along. Good food, better company," His tone was light, but his eyes stayed steady on hers.

Alyssa hesitated. The temptation of a quiet night sorting through her photos and jotting notes was strong—safe, predictable, solitary. But something in Riley's expression softened her resolve. Maybe it was the subtle warmth in his voice or the way he leaned slightly toward her, as if her answer actually mattered.

"No excuses," he said, his tone playful but firm. "You've been working hard all day. Time to take a break. Consider it part of your research—discovering how cowboys unwind after a long day."

Alyssa chuckled. "Using my job against me? That's unfair, you know."

"Sometimes you have to play dirty," Riley said with a wink, leaving no room for argument. "Meet me at the truck in ten minutes."

As Riley walked away, Alyssa stayed put, toying with the strap of her camera. She thought back to the group of giggling girls on horseback, ranking cowboys with the carefree innocence of youth. She envied them. Their ability to fully immerse themselves in the moment without second-guessing every decision, every move they made.

Could she do that? Could she let go of the questions, the overthinking, the uncertainty?

She exhaled slowly. *Yes!*

For one night, she would allow herself to do

just that. No over analyzing. No worrying about tomorrow.

With an iced tea in hand and a newfound resolve, Alyssa crossed the rodeo grounds toward the blue pickup truck, her steps lighter than they had been in a long time.

A handsome cowboy was waiting there. For her. And for tonight, that was enough.

Eleven

RILEY

THE STEAKHOUSE DOORS SWUNG OPEN, releasing a wave of warmth, laughter, and the mouthwatering aroma of sizzling steaks on the grill. Riley's hand found the small of Alyssa's back as he guided her over the threshold into the packed restaurant.

The contact sent an unexpected jolt through him, and he quickly removed his hand, suddenly aware of the intimacy of the gesture. He hadn't meant to touch her that way—it had been instinctive, the kind of casual touch he might offer anyone. But with Alyssa, it didn't feel casual at all.

"There they are," he said, nodding toward the back where several familiar faces gathered, waving to get their attention. The group had pulled several tables together, and the air buzzed with post-rodeo energy.

Riley cleared his throat as they reached the table. "Everyone, this is Alyssa. She's the reporter the Association hired for that article." His voice carried a hint of pride he couldn't quite shake.

"Pleasure to meet you, ma'am." A tall cowboy with a handlebar mustache stood and shook her hand. "I'm Hank."

"Hello, Hank. Nice to meet you."

Hank tipped his hat back slightly, studying her with a friendly curiosity that held just a hint of reservation. "Riley says you work for the paper in Bluestem. Is that right?"

"That's right," she said. "And you were in the team roping event, I think."

Hank's expression remained neutral, polite but measuring. "Yep. Me and my buddy Dale over there." He pointed to the man who sat a few chairs down from him.

"I thought I recognized that mustache," she continued, gesturing to Hank. "You two were really good out there today. I got some great shots of the action."

Dale stood and shook her hand as well, his grip firm but his smile not quite reaching his eyes. "Originally from Chicago, right? That's what I heard."

Before Alyssa could answer, a woman with a long blonde braid reached across the table to shake her hand. "I'm Bethany," she said, her voice carrying a hint of a southern drawl. "So what brings a city girl all the way out to Bluestem, Nebraska? That's quite the change of scenery."

Alyssa's smile faltered for just a fraction of a second, so brief Riley might have missed it if he hadn't been watching her so closely.

Riley felt his jaw tighten. The questions weren't subtle, and neither was the skepticism in their eyes. He knew exactly what was happening—his friends were circling the wagons, protecting him from another potential heartbreak. Part of him appreciated their loyalty, but a larger part bristled at their assumption that he needed their interference.

"Bethany. Barrel racer, right? I got some great shots of you rounding that last barrel. Your form was incredible." Alyssa smiled, her posture relaxed and confident as she settled into the chair Riley pulled out for her.

"And in answer to your question, I needed a change. My godmother Maggie owns the Gazette and offered me the position. It was the right opportunity at the right time."

Riley watched her, impressed by how smoothly she handled the interrogation. Most people would have squirmed under the scrutiny, but Alyssa seemed unfazed. She'd navigated the situation with more grace than he could've managed.

Riley watched quietly as Alyssa worked her way around the table, meeting each of his friends with a handshake and a smile. Despite being an outsider, she'd proven herself in the way that mattered most to his friends—with honesty and a connection to their world.

The conversation flowed easily as Alyssa asked thoughtful questions with genuine interest. She wasn't just making small talk; she was drawing out stories and anecdotes from the cowboys, each one more colorful than the last.

Riley noticed how even the quieter members of the group opened up to her, their faces lighting up as they told tales of past rodeos and close calls. Her journalistic instincts were obvious, but so was a warmth that Riley hadn't counted on.

He settled back in his chair, the wooden frame creaking under his weight, and took in the scene. This was his world, a place where he could relax and be himself. And somehow, Alyssa had earned her place in it.

Still, something nagged at him. What did he really know about her? He'd picked up snippets of information around town: her impressive career in Chicago, the abruptness of her move to Bluestem, her connection to Maggie.

The pieces didn't quite fit, and he found himself more and more curious about what she wasn't saying. Why would someone with her talent choose to work for a small-town newspaper? What secrets was she hiding?

"Are you planning to go to the dance tonight?" Bethany asked as they finished their meals. "It's tradition after the first day of competition."

"I hadn't really thought about it," Alyssa said, glancing at Riley. "I was just planning to review my notes and photos from today."

"Notes?" Dale exclaimed, placing a hand over

his heart in mock horror. "On a Saturday night? That's just plain wrong."

"He's right," Hank said. "If you want to capture the real spirit of the rodeo, you got to experience the whole thing—including the dance."

Riley turned to Alyssa. "So, what do you say? Would you... want to go to the dance?" He watched her closely, waiting for her response. A part of him worried she might decline, retreat back into her professional shell. Instead, she surprised him.

"I'd love to," she said, her eyes meeting his. "If you don't mind being my tour guide for a little while longer."

"I think I can manage that," he said, unable to keep the smile from his face.

The waitress appeared, setting the bill on the table. Riley reached for it at the same time as Hank, but Hank snatched it away with a grin. "I got this one," he said. "You just make sure this lady gets the full rodeo experience."

"My treat next time," Riley said, nodding his thanks to Hank. Then he stood and held out his hand to Alyssa. "All right, City Girl. Let's go put on our party clothes. We're going dancing!"

Twelve

ALYSSA

RILEY'S TRUCK rumbled to a stop, and Alyssa peered out the window. The open-air pavilion buzzed with energy, while a live band played an upbeat western tune.

Alyssa smoothed the skirt of her dress, suddenly aware of how out of place she felt. She glanced at Riley, who looked perfectly at home in his jeans and boots. He caught her eye and smiled, and some of her tension melted away.

"Ready for this?" he asked, offering his arm.

"As ready as I'll ever be," she said, though her voice wavered slightly. It had been years since she'd been to a dance of any kind. She took a deep breath and slipped her hand into the crook of Riley's elbow, the warmth of his arm seeping through his sleeve and into her palm.

He led them into the pavilion. Alyssa scanned the scene, immediately charmed by the view in front of her: couples spinning and gliding under strings of twinkling lights, the makeshift bar in one corner, drinks served in mason jars.

Riley pointed to the floor. "Dance with me?" he asked.

Alyssa hesitated. "I don't really know how—"

"I've been told I'm a pretty good teacher," Riley said with an encouraging smile. "Just follow my lead."

He laced his fingers with hers and led her onto the dance floor. Once they reached an open spot, he turned to face her, drawing her into his arms with a gentle pull, his hand settling at the small of her back. His touch was warm and firm, a gentle pressure that steadied her nerves.

"It's a simple two-step," he whispered in her ear. "One, two, three, four. Just like taking a stroll."

He continued to count out the beats, his

voice calm and patient until she found a comfortable rhythm.

"See? You're a natural." Riley twirled her lightly under his arm.

Alyssa laughed, trying to keep up with his confident steps. "I'm not, but you are. Where did you learn to dance like this?"

"Family tradition," Riley said. "I've been coming to these dances since I could walk. My dad always says there's no better way to end the week than dancing to good music with a beautiful woman in your arms."

Alyssa flushed at the compliment, a warmth spreading through her that had nothing to do with the heat of the crowded pavilion. She was aware of how close they were, of his strong arms guiding her effortlessly. Beautiful woman. The words echoed in her mind, and she felt something shift inside her.

Her usual reserve melted away, replaced by a feeling she hadn't allowed herself in years—pure joy. Riley pulled her closer, guiding her across the floor with effortless grace. Alyssa forgot to worry about where to place her feet or whether she looked awkward. She was simply there with him, moving in perfect sync as he spun them around the room.

The song ended, and Alyssa was breathless with laughter as the band launched into a slower tune. The tempo change caught her off guard, and she felt a flutter of nerves return. This was different—more intimate, more deliberate.

Riley's hand remained steady at her waist as he drew her closer. "Is this okay?" he asked softly, his eyes searching hers.

Alyssa nodded, not trusting her voice. Her heart hammered as she rested one hand on his shoulder, the other still clasped in his. The space between them narrowed until she could feel the warmth radiating from him, could catch the faint scent of his cologne mixed with the outdoors.

"You're doing great," he murmured, his breath warm against her temple as they swayed together.

The world around them seemed to fade—the other dancers, the chatter, even the music became a distant backdrop to the moment they were sharing. Alyssa was acutely aware of every point of contact: his hand splayed across her back, his thumb tracing small, unconscious circles that sent shivers down her spine. The solid strength of his shoulder beneath her palm. The way their bodies moved together as if they'd been dancing like this for years instead of minutes.

"Riley," she whispered, though she wasn't sure what she meant to say.

He pulled back just enough to look at her, his eyes dark and intense in the glow of the twinkling lights. "Yes?"

Alyssa's thoughts drifted to Trevor. She wondered what he would think of all this—of her being here, of her dancing with Riley. The grief was still there, a heavy stone in her chest, but it shared that space now with something else, something more confusing.

"Nothing," she said finally. "I just... this is nice."

"It is," he agreed, and the way he said it — low and sincere — made her breath catch.

As the song drew to a close, Riley leaned down, his lips close to her ear. "Every song they play tonight," he said, his voice sending a tremor through her, "is for you and me."

Alyssa pulled back to look at him, her eyes

wide. The declaration hung between them, tender and profound. It wasn't a grand gesture or a dramatic pronouncement—it was simple, honest, and somehow that made it all the more powerful.

"Every song?" she managed, her voice barely above a whisper.

"Every single one," he confirmed, his gaze never leaving hers.

Alyssa took a deep breath and let herself lean into Riley's arms. She'd promised herself that tonight, she would not overthink. She'd just dance.

And dance they did. Song after song, Riley kept his word. When the band played something fast, he spun her until she was dizzy with laughter. When they played something slow, he held her close, and Alyssa felt herself relaxing into his embrace, letting go of the fear and uncertainty that had been her constant companions for so long.

As the night wound down and couples began heading home, Alyssa found herself reluctant for it to end. She stood near the edge of the floor, still feeling the ghost of Riley's hand on her waist.

"Well, what did you think of your first rodeo dance?" Riley asked. He leaned against a rustic wooden beam, arms crossed, a relaxed smile playing on his lips.

"Honestly? It was the most fun I've had in a long time," she said, surprising herself with the truth of that.

"Me, too," he said, his eyes meeting hers. It was a simple exchange, but in that quiet moment, something unspoken passed between them—a promise, perhaps, of what could be, if she would just allow it to happen.

"Ready to head back?" Riley asked, glancing at his watch.

Alyssa nodded. "I guess," she said. "We both have a long day ahead of us tomorrow."

As they drove away, Alyssa took one last look at the twinkling lights in the side mirror. The evening replayed in her mind. His patience. His gentle touch. The way he'd held her during those slow dances, as if she were something precious.

They pulled into the hotel parking lot, and Riley cut the engine. "Here we are. Our home away from home," he said.

Alyssa felt a flutter of nerves as Riley came around to her side of the truck. He offered his hand, and Alyssa took it, marveling at how naturally their fingers intertwined. The warmth of his touch as he helped her down from the truck sent a spark through her that both thrilled and terrified her.

Riley walked Alyssa to her room, their footsteps echoing in the empty hallway. Neither spoke, but the silence between them felt comfortable, weighted with everything that had happened that evening.

They reached her door, and Alyssa fished her key card out of her pocket. She turned to Riley, suddenly aware of the silence between them.

"Thanks again," she said. "Tonight was lovely."

Riley smiled, but his eyes were serious. "Anytime."

Alyssa hesitated, unsure of what came next. Should she shake his hand? Say goodnight? Just disappear?

Something impulsive flickered to life inside her. Perhaps it was the way he'd held her as they danced, or the promise she'd made to herself to enjoy the night, or those words he'd whispered: every song is for you and me. Before she could talk herself out of it, she stepped forward and brushed her lips against his—just a quick, simple kiss, swift and soft as a feather.

His eyes widened. Surprise flashed across his face, and time seemed to freeze. She pulled back, her heart hammering in her chest as she registered what she had done.

"Goodnight, Riley!" she said, retreating into her room before he could stop her.

What had possessed her to do that? Alyssa pressed her fingers to her lips and laughed, recalling the surprised look on Riley's face, his eyes wide with astonishment. Had he really not seen it coming?

Alyssa took a deep breath and closed her eyes, trying to sort through the tangle of feelings inside her. Were her feelings for Riley genuine, or was the charming cowboy just a convenient distraction to help her escape her grief? And even if that was the case, was that such a terrible thing? Perhaps a small fling with a good-looking cowboy was the anecdote she needed to finally overcome her grief.

She wasn't sure what any of it meant or where it was going, but for the first time in a long while, she felt something other than numb. And it felt good. Really good.

Alyssa crossed to the bed and sank down onto the soft quilt. "Time for bed," she told herself, pushing away the temptation to think and rethink every minute of this magical night. "Your rodeo adventure isn't over yet."

Thirteen

RILEY

THE MORNING LIGHT filtered through the window blinds of the hotel dining room and cast a soft glow on the table. Riley took a sip of his coffee and felt the warmth spread through him. He looked over at Alyssa. She was studying the menu with a furrowed brow, her hair falling in loose waves around her face.

Last night kept replaying in his mind—that moment at her door, the soft press of her lips against his, the way his heart had stuttered when she pulled back with surprise in her eyes. He'd barely slept, his thoughts churning between confusion and hope.

He'd been in relationships before. With Shelby, everything had been surface-level—the right restaurants, the right events, the right image. They'd looked good together, but there'd been no depth, no actual connection. Just two people going through the motions of what a relationship was supposed to look like.

This—*whatever this was* — felt entirely different. He'd felt it in the cab of his truck yesterday, the way their voices tangled together over the radio, harmoniously off-key, her laughter catching him off-guard. Not flirting. Not routine. There'd been something genuine in it, a bright, spontaneous joy.

Later, when she sat with him and his friends, listening as they swapped rodeo stories, he saw it in her eyes: she wasn't just nodding along, waiting for her turn to speak. She was in it with them, interested in a way that rang true.

And when they'd danced—the memory of her smile, wide and easy, the way she trusted him to lead—it hadn't been about looking good, or performing for anyone. It had just been real.

This wasn't just physical attraction; it was a connection that ran deeper than anything he'd experienced before.

And that terrified him.

Because what he was feeling wasn't casual or

convenient. It was deep and real and completely overwhelming.

"Anything look good?" he asked, breaking the silence and his own spiraling thoughts.

Alyssa looked up. "I'm torn between the blueberry pancakes and the Denver omelet. What do you think?"

Riley chuckled. "Well, I'd say go for both, but then again, I've got a bull to ride later."

Alyssa smiled and returned to studying the menu. Riley fidgeted with his coffee mug, then set it down. He couldn't keep dancing around what had happened.

"Alyssa," he said softly, "about that kiss…"

She looked up, her cheeks flushing slightly. "Riley, I know what you're going to say. It was impulsive, and I shouldn't have done it. Let's just forget it happened and focus on today."

Riley blinked, surprised by her abrupt response. She wanted to forget it? The kiss that had kept him awake half the night?

"Actually …" he said, carefully searching for the right words. How could he explain what he was feeling without scaring her off? "I just wanted you to know that I had a really good time yesterday. And your kiss was the perfect ending to a perfect day. Thank you."

Alyssa's eyes widened, her fingers fidgeting with the edge of the menu.

He leaned forward, keeping his voice gentle. "I just needed to tell you that. And I want you to know that I'm not opposed to the idea of something more developing between us. If that's something you might want too."

The words hung in the air between them, vulnerable and honest. Alyssa's eyes searched his face, and he could see her processing what he'd said.

"I don't know, Riley," she said quietly. "I'm just... it's complicated for me right now."

"I know," Riley said. "And I'm not asking for anything you're not ready to give. I just wanted you to know where I stand."

She reached across the table and squeezed his hand briefly. "Thank you. And you're right. Yesterday was a really perfect day—from start to finish."

"Ready to order, folks?" The waitress's voice broke in, and Riley looked up, surprised by the interruption. He'd been so lost in their conversation, he hadn't noticed her.

"Ladies first," he said, smiling at Alyssa.

"I'll have the Denver omelet with extra cheese and hash browns," she told the waitress, closing her menu decisively.

"And I'll take the steak and eggs, medium rare," Riley said. The waitress jotted down their selections and walked away.

For a moment, they sat quietly, the clatter of dishes and low hum of conversation filling the space between them. Riley traced the rim of his coffee mug, trying to find his way back to a comfortable conversation.

"Alyssa, can I run something by you?"

She set her coffee mug down and gave him her full attention. "Of course. What's on your mind?"

Riley leaned back in his chair and ran a hand through his hair. "You know my family owns Manchester Trucking, right?"

Alyssa nodded.

"Well, my dad's pushing pretty hard for me to take over as president of the company when he retires. And I do really enjoy working with him and Katie in the office. But..." Riley trailed off, his gaze drifting to the quiet courtyard located just outside the dining room window.

"But?" Alyssa prompted gently.

"But I love the rodeo. I love the travel, the competition, the whole lifestyle."

Alyssa reached out and touched his hand, just for a moment. "Riley, this isn't your dad's life. Or your dad's decision. Do what's right for you. What makes you happy."

"I know. That's what Carter keeps telling me, too. But will ignoring my dad's wishes actually make me happy? Or will it just make me more miserable?"

Alyssa sat back in her chair and looked into his eyes. "That's always the big question about choices, isn't it? If only we had the benefit of twenty-twenty hindsight when we were making them, life would be so much simpler!"

Riley laughed at her matter-of-fact reply, a genuine, hearty laugh that echoed softly in the nearly empty dining room. He still didn't have the answers, but just talking to Alyssa made him feel a little less anxious.

"Thanks for listening," Riley said. "I really needed someone to talk to who's not involved with the family business."

"Anytime," Alyssa said. "I'm honored that you shared it with me."

"I hope you don't mind me asking," Riley said, "but how did you decide to come to Bluestem and work for Maggie? Was it a tough choice for you?"

Alyssa hesitated, then shrugged lightly. "Every choice has its challenges. Coming here was a leap of faith, but I needed a change. Sometimes we just have to take a chance and see where it leads."

Riley considered her words. Taking a chance. That was exactly what he was afraid of, yet also what he longed for.

The two of them fell into a comfortable silence, each lost in their own thoughts, as they focused on their breakfast. The hum of the hotel restaurant and the clinking of silverware created a soothing backdrop. Riley stole a glance at Alyssa, noting how her features softened when she was deep in thought. He wondered what she was mulling over. Was she thinking about his life choices or her own?

The waitress returned with the check, and Riley grabbed it before Alyssa could protest. "I've got this," he said firmly. "Consider it a thank you for acting as my sounding board this morning."

Alyssa frowned as if she wanted to object, but then nodded. "All right. Thank you."

Riley put his credit card in the small leather folder and handed it to the waitress. He noticed Alyssa looking at him as if she had something more to say. He raised an eyebrow in question.

"Riley," she said, "whatever you decide, just remember it's not set in stone. You can always change your mind. Life is a staircase of decisions, not a single path."

He let her words sink in. There was wisdom in them, a depth of understanding that he hadn't expected. "You're right. Thanks."

They walked together down the hall to the elevator, the clinking of dishes and soft murmurs of morning conversations fading behind them.

While they waited for the elevator, Riley felt a quiet contentment settle over him. They'd talked about the kiss, about possibilities, about the future—his and maybe even theirs. The uncertainty was still there, but it felt less daunting now.

The elevator dinged, pulling him back to the present.

"The rodeo starts at one this afternoon,

right? What time do you want to leave to head over there?"

Riley pressed the button for Alyssa's floor, then his. "We should probably get there before noon. Let's meet at the truck at about eleven thirty."

"All right," Alyssa said, smiling.

The elevator doors slid open, and Alyssa stepped out. "See you at the pickup," she called as the doors slid closed.

Riley sagged against the elevator wall and closed his eyes. The past twenty-four hours played on repeat in his mind. Alyssa's laughter, her genuine interest when interviewing his rodeo buddies, the way she had slowly dropped her guard around him. It all stirred something deep inside him.

He sighed, rubbing his face wearily. Alyssa was just in town for a short while, and her reasons for being here were still a mystery. But one thing was abundantly clear: when she got whatever she came for, she'd be gone, back to her real life in Chicago.

The elevator chimed, and Riley walked slowly to his room, keycard in hand. He unlocked the door to his room and entered, staring at the unmade bed, his scattered gear, and the empty coffee cup on the desk. The room felt oppressively quiet after the chatter in the dining room.

With a heavy sigh, Riley gathered his things. This rodeo performance was important—every ride counted for the season standings—but his heart wasn't in it. Not today.

He closed his eyes and imagined the ride this afternoon. The roar of the crowd, the adrenaline rush, the sheer force of the bull beneath him. It used to be enough to keep him going, to make all the sacrifices worthwhile. Now, he wasn't so sure.

He zipped his bag and glanced out the window at the clear blue sky. Whatever happened next, he needed to brace himself for it. Because the flutter he felt in his chest each time she smiled at him was a clear sign he was already halfway in love with her.

<h1 style="text-align:center">Fourteen</h1>

RILEY

THE RODEO GROUNDS buzzed with energy. The air was thick with the scent of trampled dirt and hot dogs on the grill, mingling with the occasional waft of livestock. He loved this—every chaotic, noisy, heart-pounding second of it.

Riley tightened the straps on his chaps, his hands moving automatically, guided by years of practice. His mind, however, refused to stay on the task at hand.

He searched the stands until he spotted Alyssa, her camera poised and ready. The thought of her watching made his stomach do a little flip, like the first drop on a rollercoaster.

"Manchester, you ready?" the chute boss asked.

Riley gave a curt nod, more to convince himself than anyone else. He took a deep breath and climbed the chute. Below him, the bull snorted and shifted its weight, a coiled spring of muscle and fury. Riley straddled both sides of the chute, then lowered himself slowly, giving the bull a chance to get used to his weight. He set his grip, adjusted the bells on his rope, and ran through his mental checklist: Rope tight? Check. Hand secure? Check. Balance centered? Check.

He tried to block out everything but this ride and this moment, but thoughts of his father, his future, and Alyssa teetered on the edges of his concentration. The world slowed to a crawl as he forced himself to stay present.

The gate flew open, and the bull exploded into the arena. Riley matched its every move, an intricate ballet of instinct and grit, each buck and twist a scene in an adrenaline-fueled movie.

Then, as quickly as it began, it was over. Riley dismounted and sprinted for the fence, the bull's horns slicing through empty air behind him. The crowd erupted, and Riley allowed himself a small, victorious grin.

He scanned the stands for Alyssa, but

couldn't find her. With a sigh, he unstrapped his gear and stood up, stretching his sore muscles.

"Riley! That was amazing!" Alyssa burst through the crowd and launched herself at him. She wrapped her arms around his neck and pressed her cheek against his sweat-soaked shirt.

Riley froze, not sure what to do with his hands, his body, his heart.

"You were incredible," she said, pulling back just enough for him to see the pride in her eyes.

"Nice ride, Manchester," the chute boss said. "And who's this? Your good luck charm?"

"She's a friend," Riley said, a bit too defensively.

Alyssa's cheeks flushed. "I'm a journalist, here to cover the rodeo," she said.

And don't forget that, Riley told himself. *She'll be gone before the first snowfall.*

"I see," said another cowboy, a huge grin on his face. "So if I make it through my eight seconds, do I get the same reward?"

"Sorry. Not today," said Alyssa. "My editor only allows me to give one hug per rodeo. Maybe next time!"

Hank clapped his hand on Riley's shoulder.

"Dale says me I missed the best part of your ride. Can I get an instant replay? Maybe in slow-motion?"

Alyssa smiled sweetly at Hank and reached out to tweak his handlebar mustache. "I could describe it frame by frame, but you'd probably just get jealous."

The small crowd gathered around them erupted in laughter, clearly enjoying the banter.

Riley shook his head, unable to fight the grin tugging at his lips. He had to give Alyssa credit—she wasn't backing down from the cowboys' teasing. In just a few short weeks, he'd seen her in so many lights: the committed professional who captured each moment of the rodeo with meticulous accuracy, the easygoing traveling companion who belted out country songs along with the radio, and now this mischievous, playful side that traded jabs with the cowboys he considered brothers.

He liked every one of those sides, except possibly the side that had her scaling the arena fence and falling into the ring. That memory still made his chest tighten. But even in that moment, he'd admired her determination.

Bethany's voice cut through the lingering

laughter. "So, are you two joining us for supper tonight? We're hitting up Hank's favorite barbecue joint. I earned those extra calories after my first barrel racing win of the season!"

Riley glanced at Alyssa, who tried and failed to hide a yawn behind her hand.

"We'd better pass this time," Riley said. "Maybe next time."

Bethany shrugged and adjusted her hat. "Suit yourselves. More food for the rest of us!"

Hank gave a mock salute. "Drive safe, Manchester. See you next week in Ponca."

The cowboys shrugged and offered their farewells, melting back into the crowd. Riley turned to Alyssa, who looked both relieved and a little guilty.

"You didn't have to—" she started.

"I know," he said, cutting her off, but not unkindly. "Come on. Let's go home."

THE DRIVE back to Bluestem was lit by the setting sun, turning the landscape into golden fields and long shadows. Riley's truck moved steadily along the two-lane highway, its engine humming quietly.

Alyssa dozed in the passenger seat. Her head rested against the window, and her tousled black hair made her look younger, more vulnerable.

The road stretched out before them, a ribbon of asphalt winding through the rolling plains. Riley liked this stretch, especially at sunset. It had a way of calming him, of putting things in perspective. The sky was a canvas of oranges and pinks, the sun a lazy brushstroke sinking toward the horizon. He cracked the window, letting in a breeze that carried the scent of cut hay and distant wood smoke.

Alyssa stirred but didn't wake.

Riley parked the truck outside the Whitemore Hotel and cut the engine. He looked over at Alyssa, her breathing slow and even. He hated to wake her; she looked so peaceful.

"Hey," he said, giving her a gentle nudge. "We're home."

Alyssa stirred, blinking the sleep from her eyes. She stretched and yawned, then looked around, disoriented for a moment. "Already?" she asked, her voice still thick with sleep.

"Yeah. Come on, I'll walk you up."

The evening had cooled, and crickets serenaded them as they made their way to the porch, Riley carrying her overnight case while Alyssa shouldered her camera bag.

Alyssa paused at the top of the steps and turned to face him. He stopped a step below her, bringing them eye to eye.

Riley breathed in her sweet scent, the weight of her bag anchoring him to the moment. He felt a pull, an almost magnetic force drawing him closer to her. He wanted to kiss her, to feel her lips on his once again.

"Goodnight, Riley," she said, breaking the spell. Her fingers brushed against his as she took the overnight case from him. Before he could stop her, she slipped inside, leaving him standing on the hotel porch, a mixture of longing and uncertainty swirling in his chest.

What did he feel for her? It was more than just attraction; he knew that much. Other women had drawn him in before, ignited that tug, that spark—but this was different. Alyssa had strength, determination, a way of slipping into any situation and making it work.

Was this infatuation? Maybe. But it felt deeper than that. Stronger.

And what about Alyssa? Why had she kissed him last night—hugged him today after his ride—then disappeared tonight before he could return the favor?

Riley shoved his hands into his pockets and started back toward the truck. He was exhausted, not just from the physical demands of the rodeo, but from the emotional toll of the past few weeks. Too many questions and not enough answers.

Riley opened the door of his truck and slid into the driver's seat. He leaned back and closed his eyes, letting the tension drain from his body. He knew he wouldn't find the answers tonight— not with his mind this foggy, his heart this tangled. All he could do now was get some rest and hope for a clearer head in the morning.

Fifteen

ALYSSA

THE CURSOR BLINKED at Alyssa as she stared at the blank document. She sighed, fingers hovering over the keyboard as she tried to focus on the task at hand. The article for the rodeo association was not going to write itself.

Alyssa closed her eyes and rolled her head back, willing the words to come. But instead of steer wrestlers and barrel racers, all she could see was Riley's smile, his eyes crinkling at the corners as he guided her through the two-step.

"Focus, Downing," she said, shaking her head to clear the memory.

She reached for her notebook, flipping through pages of hastily scribbled observations.

The pages transported her back to the arena—the cheers, the dust, the anticipation hanging in the air.

Her gaze shifted to the small stack of photos she had printed out for inspiration. She picked up a candid shot of Riley atop Hank's horse, hat tipped back, his grin wide and genuine. Her heart did a little flip.

"Stop it," she said, tossing the photo back down on her desk. "This is work, not a high school crush."

For the past two hours, she'd been trying to convince herself that her desire to make Riley one of the primary subjects in her article had nothing to do with the attraction she felt for him. "He is a key part of the story," she said, almost defiantly.

Lenny poked his head through her doorway. "Talking to yourself again, Chicago?"

"Just working through some writer's block," Alyssa said, a small smile tugging at her lips. "Nothing Maggie and her deadline won't cure."

She turned back to her laptop, fingers flying across the keys as she crafted a paragraph about Riley's performance. As she wrote, she wove in details about his dedication to the sport and his connection with the rodeo community.

"Keep it objective," she reminded herself, but couldn't help adding a line about the way he'd captivated the audience.

A soft knock pulled Alyssa from her writing trance.

Maggie entered, a steaming mug of coffee in each hand. The sweet scent of cinnamon and vanilla filled the room.

"Thought you might need this," Maggie said, placing one mug on Alyssa's desk. "How's the article coming?"

Alyssa's shoulders relaxed as she breathed in the aroma. "It's... getting there. Thanks, Maggie."

Maggie perched on the edge of the desk. "I can't wait to read it. You have such great instincts."

A surprised laugh escaped Alyssa's lips. "You think so? In Chicago, every single idea I pitched got dissected to death."

"Well, you're not in Chicago anymore," Maggie said.

"Don't I know it!" Alyssa took a long sip,

savoring the rich flavor. "I can't tell you how much I've enjoyed writing for the Gazette, Maggie. Getting to dive deep without twenty editors second-guessing every word... it's like breathing fresh air after being stuck in a room filled with smoke."

Maggie reached out, giving Alyssa's hand a gentle squeeze. "That's what good journalism is all about, dear. Telling the truth, not just reporting the facts. Now, get back to work ... daylight is burning!" Maggie waved and headed out the door, leaving Alyssa alone once again.

Hours later, she stretched her arms overhead, a contented sigh escaping her lips. The article was finished—a vibrant tapestry of local color and rodeo thrills, with Riley's profile as its natural centerpiece.

"I did it," she breathed, a sense of accomplishment washing over her.

She hit print, the familiar whir of the machine a comforting sound in the quiet office. As the pages emerged, Alyssa gathered them carefully, smoothing out a wrinkle here and there.

With a deep breath, she stood and walked to

Maggie's office, placing the stack of papers on her godmother's desk. A sticky note on top read simply: "For your review. - A".

As she closed the door softly behind her and strolled back to her office, she smiled as she felt the tension in her shoulders melt completely away.

HANNAH'S HEELS click-clacked down the hallway like a town crier's bell announcing her arrival. Alyssa looked up from her computer screen, where she'd been half-heartedly sorting through rodeo photos.

"Hey there, Superstar," Hannah said, coming around Alyssa's desk to peer at the pictures on the screen. "Rumor has it you've completed your literary masterpiece."

Alyssa laughed. "I don't know about that, but the article's done. It's on Maggie's desk now."

Hannah clapped her hands. "Well, that calls for a celebration! Go home, get LeAnne, and the two of you can meet me at the Rusty Spur for supper. First round's on me."

Hannah leaned in closer, a mischievous glint in her eye as she whispered, "You can tell us all about your rodeo weekend. And by that, I mean all about the ride to and from the rodeo, and all the things you did when you and Riley weren't at the rodeo!"

Alyssa coughed in surprise, nearly knocking over her coffee mug. "I—um—well," she stammered, scrambling for a deflection. She took a sip of the now lukewarm coffee, hoping that would buy her a moment to think. "The rodeo was great. I couldn't believe how friendly everyone was."

"Uh-huh," Hannah nodded. "And Riley?"

Alyssa busied herself with shuffling papers on her desk. "He's... nice. Very charismatic."

Hannah stared at her. "Oh, my goodness! You're falling for our rodeo cowboy!"

"I never said that," Alyssa said, shaking her head, but her flushed cheeks told a different story.

"You didn't have to," Hannah said. "But don't worry, your secret's safe with me."

She sat back down in the chair across from Alyssa and tilted her head thoughtfully. "For what it's worth, I think Riley Manchester is a great guy. One of the best. And believe me, in Bluestem, the good ones don't come around very often, so you need to grab him quick before someone else does."

Alyssa bit her lip and stared down at her hands. Was Hannah right? Was Riley worth the risk of another heartbreak?

"So, what do you say?" Hannah pressed. "The Rusty Spur tonight?"

Alyssa fidgeted with the corner of a notepad. After three days of intense writing, all she wanted was a quiet night at the hotel in her charming studio apartment.

"Come on," Hannah said, her voice softening. "It'll be fun. You've been cooped up in this office for three days. And I don't remember the last time LeAnne left the hotel. You two both need a night out on the town!"

Alyssa chewed on her lip. She thought about her vow to live in the moment and enjoy the journey. "Okay," she said. "Let's do it!"

"That's the spirit! I'll see you at the Rusty Spur at six!" She spun around on her heel and headed back to the front desk, humming all the way.

Alyssa shook her head and smiled. She shut

down her computer, grabbed her bag, and headed for the door. For the first time in a long while, the prospect of an evening out didn't feel like a chore. Instead, it felt like a step forward.

"Maybe," she thought, "this is what moving on feels like."

Sixteen

RILEY

RILEY STEPPED through the open doorway of the Rusty Spur, followed by Carter, their boots echoing against the polished wooden floor. The bar's dim lighting cast everything in a warm amber glow.

"Man, I'm ready for a cold one," Carter said, rolling his shoulders.

"Me, too," Riley said, his gaze scanning the room. As they headed toward the bar, Carter nudged him.

"Look who's here," he said, pointing.

Riley turned slightly, his heart skipping a beat as he spotted Alyssa sitting at a round table in the back corner of the room with LeAnne and

Hannah. "I see," he managed, though his voice felt thick.

Alyssa was laughing, looking more relaxed than he'd ever seen her. The sight of her stirred a mix of longing and nervousness deep within him. Was it strange to feel so drawn to someone he'd only known for a few weeks?

"Why don't we go say hi?" Carter said, glancing sideways at Riley, who hesitated for just a heartbeat too long.

"Sure," Riley said, trying to sound casual.

"Well, if it isn't the three prettiest gals in Bluestem," Carter said, tipping his hat. "Sitting together, just waiting for two of the handsomest guys to appear."

LeAnne scooted her chair over, making room between her and Hannah. "Yep, Cowboy. And it looks like they aren't going to show, so you two may as well take their places."

"Ouch!" Carter clutched his chest dramatically. "That hurts, LeAnne!"

"Oh, stop it! You know I'm joking. Sit here next to me and we'll let you two gentlemen buy us another round."

Carter sat down between Hannah and

LeAnne, and Riley caught the quick, almost conspiratorial glance that passed between his brother and Hannah. He didn't have to be Sherlock Holmes to recognize what game these two were playing.

"Pull up a chair, Ry," Carter said, gesturing toward the space next to Alyssa. His brother's look was part encouragement, part challenge.

With no graceful way to back out, Riley sat down. The scent of her, something light and floral, hit him immediately. He was painfully aware of how close they were sitting, their shoulders nearly touching.

Carter flagged down the waitress and ordered a couple of beers and more wine for the women. Then he leaned back in his chair. "Alyssa, how was the rodeo?" he asked. "Get some good shots of my baby brother while you were there?"

Hannah snorted. "Some? Try about a hundred. Her office desk is littered with photos of this guy."

Alyssa's cheeks flushed a delicate pink, and she ducked her head, hiding behind her hair. The sight sent a warm rush through Riley's chest.

He leaned in, his voice dropping to a conspiratorial whisper. "Don't worry, Darlin'. I know it takes a lot of tries to get one decent picture of this mug."

As the laughter bubbled up around the table, Riley's eyes found Alyssa's, and he flashed a grin intended just for her.

As Carter flirted with Hannah and LeAnne and Alyssa shared some of her highlights from the weekend, Riley sat back, content to just listen, as the stories shifted and morphed from tales of the rodeo to tales of Bluestem and some of its more charming characters. Hannah was in the middle of a humorous anecdote about Lenny when Riley caught Alyssa stifling a yawn.

"Long day?" he asked gently, nudging her shoulder.

"Long week," she admitted.

"Are you ready to go home? I'll walk with you, if you'd like." The words were out before he could second-guess himself.

"You don't need to do that."

"I want to. Can't have you getting lost out there in our big city." He grinned, trying to keep the mood light despite his heart beating double-time at the thought of being alone with her again.

Alyssa hesitated, her eyes darting from Riley to the others at the table, coming to rest on LeAnne, who was in an animated conversation with Hannah and Carter. "If you're sure it's not too much trouble," she said finally, tucking a stray lock of hair behind her ear.

"No trouble at all," Riley said, pushing back his chair.

They stood and said their goodbyes to the others, then headed for the outside.

The door of the Rusty Spur swung shut behind them with a soft thud, muffling the chatter and laughter from inside. Riley offered Alyssa his arm, and they began the six-block walk down Main Street toward the Whitemore, their footsteps tapping a steady rhythm against the old brick sidewalk. The lit street lamps cast a silvery glow across the quiet streets.

"What do you think of Bluestem so far?" he asked.

"I like it," Alyssa said, her voice thoughtful. "I mean, I grew up in Omaha, and I've lived in Chicago for the past five years. The pace here is much slower, but I'm getting used to it."

"Can I ask how you ended up in Bluestem? I mean, I know you're here to work for Maggie. But why now?" He tried to keep his tone casual but couldn't help his genuine curiosity.

She hesitated for a moment, as if trying to decide how to answer. Then, with a slight stiffening of her shoulders, she began to talk, her gaze fixed on the sidewalk in front of them.

"It's a bit of a long story," she said, drawing in a breath. "I left Chicago after..." Her voice trailed off as she bit her lip.

"After what?" he asked gently.

"Did you know I was engaged?" she asked.

"No," he said. The news should have surprised him, but it didn't. Somehow, he had guessed that her skittishness had something to do with a man.

"I was. To Trevor." She paused, and Riley felt something shift in the air between them. "Remember that song in the truck? The one I said Trevor liked?"

Riley nodded, recalling the moment—the catch in her voice, the way she'd looked out the window. He'd known then there was more to the story, but he hadn't pushed. Now she was trusting him with the rest.

"We worked at the same magazine," she continued. "Then, three years ago, we got engaged." She smiled, but there was no joy in her voice. "We made such big plans—bought a house, dreamed of a future. Then one afternoon, coming back to the office, a drunk driver hit his car. He died two days later."

Riley felt a pang in his chest, and he found himself overwhelmed by her vulnerability. He had expected heartbreak. A love gone wrong. But not this. "I'm so sorry," he whispered, his voice low. "I can't imagine how awful that was for you."

She nodded. "I felt lost afterward. Then Maggie called. She thought maybe coming here would help me find my way again."

"God bless Maggie," Riley said. "And God bless you. Starting over takes guts."

Alyssa looked at him, surprised. "Says the guy who rides bulls for a living."

He shrugged. "Riding bulls is easy. It's just holding on and hoping for the best. What you're doing—starting over, facing your grief—that's real courage."

She was silent for a moment, and Riley wondered if he'd said too much. Then she whispered, "Some people would call it running away."

"I call it surviving," he said, meeting her eyes.

"Surviving," she said, drawing out the word like she was testing its truth. Her smile told him she might actually believe him.

As they approached the hotel, Riley slowed his pace, feeling a rush of uncertainty wash over him. He wanted to kiss her, but wasn't sure if he should. What if she wasn't ready? What if he scared her away?

"Alyssa," he began, then hesitated. The porch light cast a warm glow, illuminating her face in a way that made her look almost ethereal. "I just want you to know that whatever you need—" He faltered, searching for the right words, feeling the heaviness of the moment. "You're not alone in this. I'm here if you ever need anything, even if you just want to talk."

"Thank you, Riley. That means a lot," she replied, her voice barely above a whisper.

He wanted to say more, but wasn't sure what that would be. Her heart was healing, and he feared his growing feelings might interfere with that.

"Goodnight, Riley," she said, stepping closer. For just a moment, the world narrowed to the two of them and this moment. He remembered the way she had kissed him in Scottsbluff. Did she want him to kiss her now? Was she waiting for him to make the next move?

It was tempting to lean in, to tell her how much he cared, to ask if she felt the same. But he fought against it, sensing the fragility of her heart and the journey she needed to undertake alone.

Instead, he reached out and wrapped his arms around her, pulling her into a hug. It started off tentatively, but soon deepened, lingering longer than either of them expected.

"Just remember," he whispered against her hair, the scent of her shampoo mixing with the cool night air, "I'm here, okay? No pressure. Just... friendship."

Alyssa inhaled sharply as if processing his words, then nodded slowly against his shoulder. "I'd like that," she whispered.

"Good," he said, trying to keep his tone light even as his heart raced. "Now, go get some rest. You've earned it."

With a smile, he stepped back. As she disappeared inside, he lingered a moment, wrestling with unspoken words and the feelings he'd held in check. Then he turned away, his boots echoing in the quiet night—a reminder of the road they both still had to travel.

Seventeen

ALYSSA

ALYSSA KICKED off her shoes and sank into the couch, her mind still processing the walk with Riley. She closed her eyes and allowed herself a moment to imagine what it would be like if things were simpler, if she could just dive into whatever was developing with Riley without the weight of her past holding her back.

But the weight is here, isn't it? Always here.

She pushed herself up from the couch and crossed to her bedside table where their photo sat in its silver frame. Her fingers traced Trevor's smile—the smile that had once been her whole world.

"I miss you," she whispered to the silence.

Alyssa carefully placed the photo back on the

nightstand. She moved to the window and gazed out at Main Street below, quiet now except for the occasional passing car.

Her fingers traveled to her neck—to the engagement ring that dangled on its chain. She took a deep breath and opened the clasp, sliding the ring off the chain for the first time since she'd placed it there.

The diamond caught the lamplight, sending tiny prisms dancing across the wall. She held the ring between her thumb and forefinger, feeling its weight—both physical and emotional. For so long, this ring had been her anchor to the past, to Trevor. Now it felt different somehow, as if its meaning had shifted without her permission.

The memory of Riley's words on the walk home floated back to her: "Riding bulls is easy. It's just holding on and hoping for the best. What you're doing—starting over, facing your grief—that's real courage."

Was this what courage looked like? Sitting alone in her room, holding the physical symbol of a love that had been cut short, contemplating the possibility of something new?

The warmth of Riley's arms around her lingered, even now. She had felt so safe in that embrace, so understood. She hadn't expected that—hadn't expected him. The businessman in the diner who'd scowled at her spilled coffee was nothing like the man who'd held her tonight, who'd offered friendship with no pressure, who seemed to understand exactly what she needed.

Alyssa placed the ring gently on the nightstand beside Trevor's photo, feeling a subtle shift inside her—not forgetting, not erasing, but perhaps... making room.

Her thoughts wandered, and she teetered on the edge of a light doze when her phone buzzed against the coffee table, flashing an all-too-familiar number. She stared at it for a moment, her stomach muscles clenching.

"Lyss, we need you back. The new hire isn't working out. We can't do this without you. Please, the sooner the better." Her old boss from Chicago blurted out the words before she could even say hello.

Alyssa sat up straight, surprise and a tinge of dread knotting her insides as she absorbed his plea. Her mind spun in a hundred directions at once. "Stan, I thought you said—"

"I know what I said," he interrupted, his

voice a mixture of desperation and apology. "We thought we could manage, but it's chaos without you. Just for a few months, until we find someone competent. Please!"

She bit her lip, remembering the long nights and endless deadlines at the magazine. The adrenaline, the exhaustion, the life she'd left behind. Was she really ready to go back to that?

"Alyssa, are you there?" Stan's voice crackled with impatience. "We're on a sinking ship here."

She took a deep breath, her gaze sweeping across the room to the bulletin board above her writing desk. The clippings and photos scattered there told their own story—the beekeeper and his patience with his bees, the baker whose pastries drew folks from miles around, the rodeo cowboys and cowgirls that captured a grit and spirit for a lifestyle she hadn't known existed. Bluestem had quietly seeped into her soul, its people etching themselves into her heart.

"Let me think about it," she said, her voice steadier than she felt.

"Don't take too long. We need you, Lyss." With that, the line went dead.

She put the phone down slowly, as if it were a bomb she'd just defused. The silence of her small apartment enveloped her, a stark contrast to the hustle and bustle she'd return to in Chicago.

Chicago was her past, the place where she and Trevor had built their life together. But was it also meant to be her future?

Alyssa crossed to the window again, looking down at the brick sidewalk below. Here in Bluestem, she'd found something she never expected—a sense of belonging, fulfillment in the everyday stories, joy in writing about people who mattered. Her career had always been her anchor, yet here it was more like the sail, guiding her toward stories with purpose.

And then there was Riley. Patient, kind Riley, who made her feel seen and valued. Who made her laugh and challenged her to embrace life again. If she went back to Chicago, whatever was blooming between them would wither before it had a chance to grow. But if she stayed...

The choice before her was more than just Chicago versus Bluestem, career versus small-town life. It was about choosing between the familiar comfort of her past and the uncertain promise of her future. It was about deciding whether she was brave enough to open her heart to the possibility of new love.

Alyssa picked up the camera from her desk—the one Trevor had given her all those years ago—and cradled it in her hands. Memories of their life together flooded back, bittersweet and precious. But as she held the camera, she realized it wasn't just a reminder of what she'd lost. It was also a reminder of Trevor's gift to her—his encouragement to see the world, to capture its beauty, to tell stories that mattered.

With a sigh, Alyssa gently set the camera down, recognizing it as another symbolic act of release. She didn't have all the answers yet. She didn't know whether she'd stay in Bluestem or return to Chicago, whether she'd give her relationship with Riley a real chance or let it remain a beautiful what-if.

But for the first time since Trevor's death, her heart was ready to face the questions. And maybe, just maybe, that was enough for now.

Eighteen

RILEY

RILEY STOOD in the main office of Manchester Trucking. Truck photos lined the walls—a visual timeline of the company's growth. The polished oak front desk was weathered and worn from years of use. This was his father's world, the world he wanted Riley to take over, yet it felt as confining to him as a cage.

Charles Manchester, his father, stood behind the front desk, flipping through a ledger with the practiced ease of a man who'd spent a lifetime in the business. His graying hair and weathered face spoke of years of hard work, but his eyes still held the fire of a man who wasn't ready to slow down.

"Dad, we need to talk," Riley said, squaring

his shoulders. His voice was firm but not confrontational.

Charles looked up from his work. "About what, Son?"

Riley shifted his weight, suddenly aware of how the floor creaked beneath his boots. "About the company. About my future."

Charles closed the ledger with a soft thud and crossed his arms, leaning against the desk. The wood groaned slightly under his weight. "I'm listening."

"I know you want me to take over when you retire," Riley said, choosing his words carefully. "But the trucking business... it's not where my heart is. You know that."

The clock on the wall ticked loudly in the silence that followed. A phone rang in another office, then stopped.

"You don't have to love it, Riley. You just have to take care of it. It's your responsibility." His father's tone was even but unyielding.

Riley ran a hand through his hair, the frustration building. "What about Kate? She's already managing the day-to-day operations here at Bluestem. Why can't she step in as CEO of the entire operation?"

Charles's eyes narrowed. "Because I chose you, that's why."

"That's not fair, Dad." Riley's voice rose as he gestured toward the window where trucks were being loaded in the yard. "It's not fair to me and it's not fair to Kate. The rodeo—"

"The rodeo is a young man's game," Charles cut in, tapping his fingers against the desk for emphasis. "You can't ride bulls forever, Riley. What happens when you're too old, or worse, when you get injured? You need something stable, something you can rely on."

Riley clenched his fists, feeling the calluses on his palms. "I know, Dad. But the future you envision for me isn't the one I see for myself."

Charles uncrossed his arms and stood tall, the fire in his eyes burning brighter. "So what is your plan, then? Ride bulls until your body gives out? You need to think long-term, Riley. About settling down, about a family."

The mention of family brought Alyssa immediately to mind—the way she nibbled on her lip when she was taking a photo, the way she felt in his arms when they danced, the touch of her lips on his when she surprised him with that kiss.

"Settling down," Riley repeated, more to

himself than to his father. "Is that what this is really about?"

"It's about making smart choices, Riley. About creating a life that's sustainable."

Riley nodded, rubbing the back of his neck. "I know you're right, Dad. I just need more time to figure out what that looks like, for me."

Charles nodded, though it was unclear whether it was a nod of agreement or resignation. "I'm not hanging up my hat just yet. You've got a few months to decide. But remember, this door won't always be open for you."

Riley exhaled, a mixture of relief and ongoing tension. "I know, Dad."

As he turned to leave, Charles called out to him. "Riley, one more thing."

Riley paused, his hand on the doorknob, and looked back. His father stood framed against the window, sunlight outlining his silhouette, making him appear a bit more human, a bit more vulnerable.

"Don't wait too long to make your decision," Charles said. "Whether it's about the business, the rodeo, or that gal Carter says you're sweet on. Sometimes not choosing is the worst choice of all."

Nineteen

ALYSSA

Alyssa sat at her desk at the Gazette, the hum of the old fluorescent light a familiar backdrop to her concentration. She was deep into editing her feature about a local quilter when her office phone rang.

Her eyes widened as she saw the name on the caller ID: Carter Manchester. With a mix of curiosity and apprehension, Alyssa answered. "Carter? Is everything okay?"

Carter's usually teasing voice crackled with tension. "It's Riley. He got trampled pretty bad at the rodeo in Ponca. We're at the hospital in Sioux City."

Alyssa's heart lurched. "Bad? How bad is bad?"

"They think he's got a concussion, a dislocated shoulder, and a couple of broken ribs. They're still running tests to make sure nothing else is going on, but... he's banged up pretty good." Carter's words tumbled out. "I just thought you'd want to know."

Alyssa's fingers dug into the edge of her desk. A stack of photos slid off the corner and scattered across the floor. She ignored them.

Images of Riley flashed through her mind: the way he cocked his head to grin at her, the sound of his voice as they belted out tunes in his old pickup truck, her hand tucked securely in his when they danced. And now he was lying in a hospital bed, hurt, maybe worse. She swallowed hard, her throat dry.

"Thanks for letting me know," she managed, her voice unsteady. "Do you think he'll be... okay?"

The pause on the other end of the line was just long enough to be ominous. "We're hoping so. The doctor just came in. I've got to go. I'll keep you posted."

As she hung up, Alyssa's gaze fell on the half-finished article on her screen. The words blurred, suddenly insignificant in the face of this new reality. Riley was hurt. Really hurt. Nothing else seemed to matter.

The door creaked open, and Hannah walked in with a stack of papers. "Hey, Lyss, I just—" She stopped. "What's wrong?"

Alyssa looked up, her mouth opening but no words coming out.

Hannah set her papers down and moved closer. "Hey, talk to me. You look like you've seen a ghost."

"Carter Manchester just called," Alyssa said, her voice barely above a whisper. "Riley's in a hospital in Sioux City."

Hannah's eyes widened, and she squeezed Alyssa's arm. "What happened?"

"A bull trampled him. That's all I know." Alyssa's voice caught as she pressed her fingertips against her eyelids, willing the pressure to stop the tears that threatened to spill over.

"Do you want to go to Sioux City?" Hannah asked.

Alyssa hesitated, her thoughts in a jumble. She remembered the unexpected comfort and safety she felt when he'd hugged her, the spark of attraction that made her pulse quicken, the bittersweet ache of longing she felt when she danced with him. Just as vivid was the memory of the last day she spent with Trevor, holding his hand as he lay in the hospital bed, the room filled with the smell of antiseptic and the sound of beeping machines. The helplessness, the unbearable pain of knowing she was losing him, and there was nothing she could do.

"I don't know," she said. "I'm not even family. Would it be weird if I showed up?"

"Carter called you, remember? So, no, it won't be weird." Hannah grabbed Alyssa's purse from the coat rack and placed it firmly on the desk. "I'm driving you to Sioux City. Right now."

"But—" Alyssa gestured weakly at her computer screen.

"No buts," Hannah said, her voice firm. "You need to be there, and I'm not letting you go alone. Besides, it's not every day I get to play chauffeur."

Maggie appeared in the doorway, her silver hair slightly disheveled. "What's going on? I heard raised voices."

"Riley's in the hospital in Sioux City," Hannah said. "I'm taking Alyssa to see him."

Maggie crossed the room and pulled Alyssa into a gentle hug. Then she turned to Hannah.

"You two get going. Lenny and I can handle things here."

"Are you sure?" Alyssa asked, her voice small and uncertain.

Maggie nodded, her smile reassuring. "Absolutely. Your place is with Riley right now." She patted Hannah's shoulder. "Take good care of our girl, okay?"

"You can count on me," Hannah said, already guiding Alyssa toward the door. "Come on. Let's get you to Sioux City."

FIFTEEN MINUTES LATER, Alyssa and Hannah were in Hannah's Subaru, heading out of town. Rain dotted the windshield as they passed rolling fields that stretched toward the gray horizon. Alyssa stared out the window, her thoughts miles away with Riley.

"He's going to be okay," Hannah said, breaking the silence. "You know that, right?"

Alyssa turned to look at her. "How do you know?"

Hannah gave a small, sad smile. "I don't. But

sometimes you have to believe the best, even when you're scared."

Alyssa nodded, but her mind continued its relentless spiral. She'd let her guard down, allowed herself to care for Riley more than she'd intended. And now, faced with the possibility of losing him, she realized just how much he meant to her.

When they pulled into the hospital parking lot, Alyssa's stomach churned. The building loomed ahead, its sterile white walls and bright lights a stark contrast to the warmth of the open road. The automatic doors slid open with a mechanical hiss, and the smell of antiseptic hit her immediately, sharp and clinical. Memories rushed back—the long halls, the beeping monitors, the way Trevor's hand felt cold in hers. She clenched her fists, willing herself to stay grounded.

"Come on," Hannah said, touching Alyssa's elbow gently. She guided her toward the reception desk where a woman with graying hair worked at a computer. Alyssa looked around, her mind a swirl of past and present. She remembered sitting in Trevor's room, hoping against hope that the next doctor who came in would bring good news. A hope that died there, in that room, holding Trevor's hand.

Hannah spoke to the receptionist. Alyssa didn't catch the exchange; her eyes had locked onto a stretcher being wheeled through a set of double doors, the patient hooked up to various tubes and monitors. The scene played out in slow motion, and she felt a growing knot in her stomach.

"He's in room 312," Hannah said, pulling Alyssa toward the elevators. "Let's go."

The elevator ride was silent, Alyssa's reflection in the metal doors showing a pale face with wide, frightened eyes. Her heart pounded against her ribs as they stepped out onto the third floor.

The corridor stretched before them, quieter than the lobby below. Nurses moved efficiently between rooms, their soft-soled shoes barely making a sound on the polished floor. A doctor stood at a nurses' station, reviewing a chart and speaking in low tones.

"You okay?" Hannah asked, squeezing Alyssa's hand.

Alyssa nodded, though her legs felt like they might give way. Each step brought them closer to room 312, and with each step, her anxiety mounted. What if he were unconscious? What if he was in pain? What if he didn't want to see her?

They stopped outside Room 312, the door slightly ajar. Alyssa's hand hovered over the handle, trembling. She took a breath—shallow, insufficient—and pushed the door open.

The room was dim, curtains drawn. And there, in the hospital bed, lay Riley.

He was so still. So pale. An IV line snaked from his arm to a bag hanging beside the bed. Monitors beeped in a steady rhythm, tracking his vitals with cold precision. His chest rose and fell beneath the thin hospital blanket, but his eyes were closed, his face slack with unconsciousness.

The antiseptic smell intensified, wrapping around Alyssa like a suffocating blanket.

Trevor's hand, cold and limp in hers. The doctor's voice, somber and final: "I'm sorry. We did everything we could." The monitor's steady beep suddenly flatlining into one long, terrible tone that seemed to go on forever.

Alyssa's breath caught in her throat. The room tilted. Her vision narrowed to a tunnel, with Riley's still form at the center, and all she could feel was the crushing weight of Trevor's last hours pressing down on her chest.

"Alyssa?" Hannah's voice sounded distant, muffled.

She couldn't do this. She couldn't stand here and watch another man she cared for slip away. The beeping monitors, the sterile smell, the pale stillness of Riley's face—it was all too much, too familiar, too unbearable.

A sound escaped her lips, something between a gasp and a sob. She stumbled backward, her hand flying to her mouth. "I can't—" The words came out strangled.

As she turned toward the door, a weak voice rasped from the bed. "Alyssa?"

She froze, her back to him, her heart shattering. He was awake. He'd seen her.

"Alyssa?" His voice was rough with pain and confusion.

Every instinct screamed at her to turn around, to go to him, to take his hand. But her feet wouldn't move forward. They couldn't.

"I'm sorry," she whispered, so quietly she wasn't sure he could hear. "I'm so sorry."

Without turning around, without meeting

his eyes, she fled the room, leaving his whispered plea hanging in the sterile air behind her.

The hallway blurred as she ran, her boots echoing against the linoleum. Behind her, she heard Hannah calling her name, but she couldn't stop. The walls pressed in, the fluorescent lights too bright, the antiseptic smell burning her nostrils.

She burst through the stairwell door, her hands shaking as she gripped the railing. Her legs carried her down, down, away from the third floor, away from Riley's voice calling her name, away from the beeping monitors and the memories that threatened to drown her.

She rushed through the exit doors and stumbled into the parking lot. The rain had picked up, cold droplets hitting her face, mingling with the tears she hadn't realized were falling. She pressed her palms against her knees, gulping air that wouldn't seem to fill her lungs.

The asphalt was slick beneath her boots. She heard the hospital doors open behind her, heard Hannah's footsteps approaching.

"Lyss—"

"I can't do this," she whispered, her voice

breaking. "I thought I could, but I can't. We have to go. We have to leave."

For a moment, Hannah hesitated, her green eyes searching Alyssa's face. Then she sighed and nodded. "If that's what you want." She wrapped her arm around Alyssa's shoulders and guided her toward the car.

Alyssa moved on autopilot while her mind remained trapped in that hospital room. The passenger door clicked open, and she slid inside, the familiar scent of Hannah's vanilla air freshener doing nothing to calm the storm raging inside her chest.

She pressed her hands to her knees, forcing in shaky breaths that never seemed to fill her lungs. "He needed me," she whispered. "He called my name, and I—" Her throat closed.

Hannah touched her shoulder, but Alyssa couldn't look at her. "When Trevor was in that hospital, I stayed. Every hour, every breath, I stayed until there was nothing left to hold onto."

She swiped at her tears, rain and salt mixing on her skin. "I told myself it would be okay. That I could handle this. But the second I saw Riley like that..." She took a breath that hitched in her chest.

For a long moment, neither of them spoke. The only sounds were the rain and the faint swish of the wipers.

"I hate that I left him," Alyssa whispered. "But I can't walk back in there, Hannah. I just—can't."

Hannah's expression softened. "Then we'll go," she said.

Alyssa nodded, the motion small and unsteady. "Thank you," she said, her voice breaking on the word.

As Hannah eased the car out of the parking lot, the hospital lights faded in the rain-streaked mirrors. Guilt settled deep in Alyssa's chest—heavier than the storm, heavier than the fear. Riley was the one who'd been trampled, but she couldn't shake the feeling that she was the one who would never recover from this fall.

Twenty

ALYSSA

As the car rolled down the highway toward Bluestem, Alyssa leaned her head against the window, watching the Nebraska landscape blur past. Rain streaked across the windshield as the wipers dragged rhythmically across the glass. Fields of corn and wheat stretched endlessly on either side, their colors muted by the gray afternoon light.

"You're awfully quiet," Hannah said, adjusting the wipers. "Do you want to talk about what happened back there?"

Alyssa turned her head, her cheek still resting against the cool glass. "What do you want me to say?"

"Something," Hannah said, flicking on the turn signal as they passed a slow-moving truck. "Anything about what's going on in that brain of yours. You've barely said two words since we left the hospital."

Alyssa sighed, tracing a raindrop's path down the window with her fingertip. "It's just... seeing him lying in that hospital bed, Hannah." She closed her eyes, the image of Riley, so pale against the white pillows, searing itself into her memory. "It was all too familiar. The sounds, the smells... it brought everything back."

Hannah waited silently, her eyes occasionally flicking from the road to Alyssa.

Alyssa took a shaky breath and continued, her voice barely above a whisper. "His whole life is one big risk. Rodeos, ranching... it's dangerous. What I saw today could happen again, and it could be so much worse."

"What are you saying?" Hannah asked, slowing as they approached a flashing red light.

The words caught in Alyssa's throat. Her chest tightened, and suddenly she couldn't breathe. The dam she'd been holding back since she fled Riley's hospital room finally broke.

"Pull over," she gasped. "Hannah, please, just pull over."

Hannah immediately steered onto the shoulder, gravel crunching under the tires. Before the car had fully stopped, Alyssa's body convulsed with sobs—deep, wrenching sounds that seemed to come from somewhere primal and raw.

"I'm so sorry, Hannah." The words came out broken, punctuated by gasping breaths. "I just... I couldn't. I couldn't stay in that room. I couldn't—" Another sob cut her off.

Hannah reached over and pulled her into an awkward embrace across the console. "It's okay. Just breathe. You're okay."

But Alyssa wasn't okay. She fumbled in her purse for her phone, her hands shaking so badly she nearly dropped it twice. Through blurred vision, she scrolled to Carter's number.

"What are you doing?" Hannah asked gently.

"I have to—I need to talk to Carter." Her voice cracked as the call connected.

"Carter? It's Alyssa." She could barely get the words out through her tears. "I'm so sorry, I had to leave. I just couldn't... Please, tell Riley I'm thinking about him and I'll call when I can."

Carter's voice on the other end was warm, understanding. She couldn't make out all his words through her own crying, but his tone was enough. When she ended the call, she let the phone fall into her lap and pressed her palms against her eyes.

They sat there on the side of the highway for several minutes, rain drumming on the roof, until Alyssa's breathing finally steadied.

Hannah pulled back onto the highway, and they drove in silence for a moment, save for the slap of tires on wet asphalt. Soon they passed the "Welcome to Bluestem" sign, its cheerful blue letters a stark contrast to Alyssa's mood, and Hannah turned onto Main Street. The familiar storefronts of Bluestem slid past, windows glowing warmly against the gray day.

"I'm terrified," she whispered, staring out at the rain-soaked streets. "With Riley, it feels like I'm walking the same path I did with Trevor, and we all know how that ended." Her eyes met Hannah's. "Maybe it's just easier to run away before things get too deep."

Hannah's gaze was full of compassion. Rain fell harder, drumming against the roof of the car.

"Is running away really easier? Or does it just feel safer in the moment?"

Alyssa wrapped her arms around herself. She knew the answer, but admitting it was something else entirely. Instead, she switched subjects. "And then there's that call from Stan..."

Hannah's eyebrows shot up. "Stan? Who's Stan?"

"My old boss from the magazine." Alyssa straightened in her seat, her professional persona slipping into place like a comfortable mask. "He wants me back. Says the place is in chaos without me."

"Chaos? Really?" Hannah finally asked.

Alyssa laughed, and even to her own ears, the sound was hollow. "Well, Stan can be dramatic, but it does make me wonder if it's time to go back."

"Is that what you want?" Hannah asked, her voice gentle as she parked in front of the White-more. "To go back to Chicago?"

Alyssa stared at her hands. "A part of me misses the excitement of Chicago, the buzz of the big city. But then..."

Her voice trailed off, and Hannah finished

the thought for her. "But then there's Riley. And Bluestem."

Hannah reached out and squeezed her hand. "You do what's right for you. But don't let the past rob you of the future."

ALYSSA KICKED off her tangled sheets and rolled onto her back. The familiar sounds of Bluestem filtered through the open window—an owl hooting, leaves rustling in the night breeze, the distant bark of a dog. She stared at the ceiling, watching shadows dance across it as a car passed on the street below.

Her conversation with Hannah replayed in her mind. Hannah made it sound so simple—be brave, live in the present. But the weight of the past three years pressed down on her chest like a physical thing. Hannah meant well, but she didn't understand. How could she?

Alyssa turned onto her side and looked at the framed photograph on her bedside table. It was the only picture she'd brought with her, a snapshot of her and Trevor at the lake, both of them grinning stupidly at the camera.

Trevor — vibrant, alive, invincible Trevor— until he wasn't.

The memory of him in that hospital bed crashed over her like a wave. The ventilator. The machines. The awful, hollow sound of the doctor's voice saying there was nothing more they could do. She'd held his hand as the monitors went silent, one by one, until there was nothing left but the terrible quiet.

And today, seeing Riley in that hospital bed —the white sheets, the beeping monitors, the antiseptic smell—it had all come rushing back. Her body had known before her mind caught up: this is how it starts. This is how you lose everything.

A tear slipped down her cheek and onto the pillow.

Riley wasn't Trevor. She knew that. But Riley was a bull rider, a rancher, a man who threw himself into danger every time he climbed onto the back of a bull.

She couldn't do it. She wouldn't survive that kind of loss again.

A sob caught in her throat. She pressed her fist against her mouth to muffle the sound.

Riley deserved someone whole, someone

who could watch him chase his dreams without falling apart. Someone who could be strong when he needed strength, not someone who fled hospital rooms in a blind panic.

She was too broken for him. Too damaged. Too afraid.

Moving back to Chicago wasn't running away—it was the kindest thing she could do for both of them. Better to end it now, before they were in too deep, before the inevitable happened and she was destroyed all over again.

Alyssa sat up and pushed her hair back from her face. Moonlight slipped through the gap in her curtains, casting a silver path across the wooden floor. She padded to the window and pulled the curtains aside.

Bluestem lay quiet and still, so different from Chicago's constant hum of activity. She'd come here to escape, to heal, not to risk her heart again. Yet somehow, without meaning to, she'd fallen for a man whose life was a constant reminder of the fragility she couldn't bear to face again.

She pressed her forehead against the cool glass.

As the first hint of dawn lightened the

eastern sky, Alyssa made her decision. She lay down and closed her eyes, a sense of resignation settling over her like a heavy blanket. She had no choice. She had to protect her heart, even if it meant saying goodbye to the one man she knew for certain she could love again.

Twenty-One

RILEY

RILEY LAY on the bed in his room, the familiar scent of the ranch slipping through the open window. The pain in his side throbbed with each breath, a stubborn reminder that cracked ribs heal on their own time, not his.

Even sitting up too fast sent a sharp ache radiating through his chest. The doctor had warned him to take it slow, to give his body the four to six weeks it needed, but patience had never been his strong suit.

He traced a finger along the quilt's worn seams, his thoughts drifting to Alyssa. Three weeks had passed since the accident—one in the hospital, two more confined to the ranch. No visits. No calls. Not even a text.

For the first week, he'd felt sorry for himself, nursing his wounded pride alongside his broken body. Why hadn't she come? Carter said she'd been at the hospital that first day, but she'd left before Riley had truly regained consciousness. The silence that followed had stung.

But lying here day after day had given him time to think. And remember. That night at the Rusty Spur, when he'd walked her home, she'd told him about Trevor. About the accident. He'd seen the pain in her eyes, heard the tremor in her voice. And he'd promised her friendship—promised to be there when she needed him.

He'd been so focused on his own pain that he'd ignored what it must have cost her to even walk through those hospital doors. She'd tried. For him, she'd faced her worst nightmare. And when it became too much, when the memories overwhelmed her, she'd left. Could he really blame her?

Riley closed his eyes, guilt washing over him. She'd needed him to reach out, to let her know he understood why she couldn't be there, to let her know he was going to be fine. Instead, he'd waited for her to come to him, adding his silence to whatever burden she was already carrying.

A firm knock on the door interrupted his thoughts. "You decent?" his father called through the door, already turning the doorknob before Riley could answer.

Riley pushed himself up against the headboard, hiding a wince. Charles Manchester stepped inside, checking his watch as if visiting his son was just one more item on his to-do list that day. The habit was so ingrained, Riley doubted his father even knew he was doing it.

"You look a little better," Charles said, settling himself in the chair by the bed. "Up for a trip to the office tomorrow? Nothing strenuous, just some invoices that need sorting."

Riley forced a smile. "I was hoping you were sending me out to fix fence. Get some fresh air."

"Carter's got the ranch and its fences firmly under control, but those ledgers are piling up." Charles leaned back in his chair and crossed his arms, his frustration clearly visible.

"I'll see how I'm feeling," Riley said, keeping his tone casual even as he felt his jaw tighten.

Charles stood and took two steps toward the door before stopping, his hand resting on the doorframe. For a moment, something softer crossed his face. "Lying around, feeling sorry for yourself isn't going to fix anything. Time to get back on your feet." He left, boots clicking down the hallway, the partially open door a silent invitation.

The silence that followed pressed down on Riley's shoulders, heavy with thirty years of his father's plans and expectations. He shifted to reach for his water glass and froze as pain shot through his side, sharp enough to make his vision blur momentarily.

When the pain subsided, Riley stared at the lone light on the ceiling. Dad was right about one thing—feeling sorry for himself wasn't helping anything. And it certainly wasn't helping Alyssa.

RILEY EASED himself into a wooden rocking chair on the wrap-around porch. In his good hand, a mug of coffee slowly cooled. The morning air carried the scent of dew-soaked alfalfa and the distant hint of cattle.

He took a slow, deliberate breath, ignoring the pain in his ribs. His thoughts circled back to his bull-riding accident and how close he'd come to dying that day. He could still hear the crowd's gasp, feel the dirt in his mouth, see the flash of hooves perilously close to his head.

He flexed the fingers of his left hand, now cradled in a sling. The doctors had been clear: he was lucky to escape with just a concussion, a dislocated shoulder, and a few cracked ribs. Lucky. That word gnawed at him. How many more times could he count on luck to save him?

For the first time in his life, something hadn't come easily. He'd always been successful at whatever he'd set his mind to: sports, school, business, even bull riding. His breakup with Shelby had been easy too. When she was done, so was he. No hard feelings, no looking back.

But this accident had stripped away that illusion of invincibility. He couldn't just will his ribs to heal faster or charm his way out of the pain. Some things require patience. Some things take time. And some things—no matter how badly you want them—are simply not meant to be.

The realization settled over him like the morning dew on the pasture. He'd been trying to have it all: the rodeo career, the vice president position at Manchester Trucking, the freedom to drift between two worlds without fully commit-ting to either; one foot in the boardroom, the other in the dirt, never fully belonging to either world.

But life didn't work that way. Not really. Eventually, you had to make a choice.

A soft breeze rustled the leaves of the old oak in the front yard. Riley sipped his lukewarm coffee and grimaced at the bitter taste. He set the mug down on a small wooden table, its surface scarred from years of use.

The screen door creaked, and Riley turned to see Carter step onto the porch. His older brother wore the weary look of a man who'd been up since before dawn.

Carter was the spitting image of their father, right down to the stern set of his jaw and the deep furrow in his brow. But the warmth in his smile and the teasing gleam in his eyes, even when he was tired, came straight from their mother.

Carter took a seat on the porch swing, its chains groaning under his weight. The two brothers sat in silence for a moment, taking in the morning together. Riley marveled at how different they were, yet how well they understood each other. Where Riley was restless and searching, Carter was steady and sure.

"How's it feeling today?" Carter asked, pointing to Riley's shoulder, his concern obvious despite his casual tone.

Riley attempted a half-smile. "Still attached. Could be worse."

"You scared us, you know. That bull was a monster."

"Yeah." Riley stared at the distant pasture. "Could've been my last ride."

Carter's eyes narrowed slightly, his jaw tightening as he stared at Riley. The words hung between them, heavy in the quiet morning air.

Riley shifted uncomfortably in his chair, the pain in his ribs reminding him why they were having this conversation. He looked over at Carter. "I'm not sure this is how I want to spend the next ten to twenty years of my life."

Carter studied him, the swing swaying gently beneath him. "You having second thoughts about traveling the circuit?"

"More like accepting reality," Riley said, leaning back carefully. "I've been lucky so far, but luck runs out. I don't want to be an old cowboy with nothing more to show for it than some buckles and a pile of medical bills."

Carter rubbed his chin. "So you're going to take Dad up on his offer? Become president of the company when he retires?"

Riley pictured himself drowning in paperwork and spreadsheets. "The thought of sitting behind a desk and balancing spreadsheets for the rest of my life terrifies me more than being an old, broken down cowboy. Besides, we both know that's Kate's dream—not mine. Dad's just too blind to see that."

Carter leaned back, the porch swing creaking with the motion. "You're right about Dad, but he just wants what he thinks is best. He believes the company will give you stability, a future."

"Stability and a future," Riley repeated. "I get that. But it's not my future—not my dream."

"So, if you're not going to ride bulls and you're not taking over the company, what's the plan, little brother? You've got that look in your eye."

Riley leaned forward, his pain forgotten, at least for the moment. "While I was in the hospital, I had an idea. It's not just about what I want to do for the next decade or two. It's about building something that matters—with you."

Carter's eyebrows shot up. "I'm listening."

Riley took a breath. "I want to start a rodeo school. Here. At the ranch." His good arm animatedly gestured toward the open fields visible from the porch. "We've got the space, and I've got the experience. I know what it takes to be successful in the arena, and I know how to keep a business organized and afloat."

He paused, glancing at Carter with a hopeful grin. "Maybe we could even become stock contractors—raising and training bulls for the rodeo circuit. It would be a way to stay connected to the rodeo world without risking my neck every week. What do you think? Would you want to partner with me on this?"

Carter leaned back and took a long drink of coffee. "That's a pretty big shift, Ry. It's not like you to stay put for long. Are you sure this is what you want? It's a lot of responsibility."

Riley nodded, the conviction growing stronger with each passing moment. "Yeah, I am. I've spent so much time running—either toward the rodeo or away from Dad's business.

It's time I stayed in one spot and built something of my own. Something real."

A slow smile spread across Carter's face, his eyes crinkling at the corners. "I like it. It's got potential." He nodded, rubbing his chin thoughtfully. "And I reckon Dad might even come around to the idea, once he gets over being mad."

Riley couldn't help but laugh. "Maybe. Eventually. Dad's just going to have to come to terms with the fact that Kate's not merely bossy; she's got what it takes to be the boss."

"We could use the north pasture for the training grounds," Carter said, his practical nature already kicking in. "And that old barn by the creek? We could fix it up, turn it into a classroom space."

Riley nodded, his thoughts spinning as the two of them continued to throw out one idea after another. For the first time since the accident, he felt a sense of purpose that had nothing to do with proving himself and everything to do with building a future.

But even as excitement coursed through him, one thought kept returning. Alyssa. He wanted to see her, to tell her about this new idea. To let her know he was going to be okay. To apologize for not reaching out sooner.

And more than that—he needed to tell her he understood. That he knew why she'd left the hospital that day. That he wasn't angry or hurt. That her trying to be there at all meant everything to him.

He loved her. The realization hit him with the same force as that bull three weeks ago, stealing his breath just as effectively. He loved her courage, her kindness, the way she'd faced her fears just to be there for him. He loved the life he could imagine building with her—not the reckless, scattered existence he'd been living, but something solid and true.

But Alyssa probably wasn't ready to hear that yet. Her wounds were still raw, still healing. Her heart needed the same patience as his battered ribs—the long, slow kindness of time.

What she needed to hear was that he was okay. That she didn't need to carry guilt for leaving the hospital. That he understood, and he was sorry for not telling her that sooner.

Riley stood, his chair scraping against the wooden boards. The sudden movement sent a sharp stab through his ribs that stole his breath.

He gripped the porch railing with his good hand, waiting for the wave of pain to pass.

"Whoa there, Cowboy." Carter was on his feet in an instant. "Where do you think you're going?"

"To town. I need to see Alyssa."

"It's been three weeks, Ry." Carter's voice carried a note of caution. "You sure now's the right time?"

Riley met his brother's eyes. "No, it's *not* the right time. The *right* time was three weeks ago. I should have called her that first day I was coherent. But I can't wait any longer. She tried, Carter. She walked into that hospital for me, even though it must have terrified her. And I've let her think I didn't appreciate that, didn't understand what it cost her."

He turned toward the door, each step a reminder of what that bull had done to him. His ribs screamed their protest, but he kept moving. "I promised her friendship. I promised to be there when she needed me. Instead, I've been lying here feeling sorry for myself while she's been dealing with her fears alone."

Inside, the ranch house was quiet. He made his way down the hallway to his room, Carter trailing behind him. Riley grabbed his phone from the nightstand, his thumb already pulling up her contact.

The phone rang once. Twice.

Then her voicemail kicked in, her voice bright and professional: "Hi, you've reached Alyssa Downing. I can't take a call right now, but leave me a message and I'll get back to you as soon as I can."

The beep sounded in his ear, hollow and final.

"Alyssa, it's Riley. I—" He stopped, his throat tight. What could he say in a message that would make up for three weeks of his silence? " His voice softened. "I'm coming to town. I'll see you soon."

He ended the call and stared at the phone in his hand. The screen dimmed, then went dark.

"Straight to voicemail?" Carter asked from the doorway.

Riley nodded, already reaching for his truck keys on the dresser.

Concern etched lines across Carter's forehead. "You're in no condition to drive. Those ribs—"

"Will heal whether I'm lying in bed or sitting

in a truck." Riley moved toward the door, each step deliberate. "I've spent three weeks being patient with my body. Now I need to stop being patient about this."

Carter crossed his arms. "Then I'm driving you."

"No." Riley shook his head. "You've got work to do here. The ranch doesn't run itself."

"Riley—"

"I'll be fine, Carter. It's a twenty-minute drive, not a marathon." Riley softened his tone. "I need to do this. I need to show her I'm okay, that I'm strong enough to come to her when he needs me."

Carter studied him for a long moment, then sighed. "All right. But you call me when you get there. And if those ribs give you any trouble—"

"I'll pull over." Riley managed a smile. "I promise."

With a determined wince, Riley hobbled out of the house and down the front porch steps, gripping the railing for support. Each step sent a jolt through his side, but he kept moving.

He swung open the truck's door and gingerly eased himself inside, his injured shoulder protesting the movement. The steering wheel felt foreign in his good hand, and the simple act of turning the key made him grit his teeth against the pain.

But none of it mattered. Not the cracked ribs, not the dislocated shoulder, not the doctor's orders to rest.

He threw the truck into gear, gravel crunching under the tires as he headed toward town—and Alyssa. He needed to tell her about the rodeo school, about his decision to build something lasting. He needed to apologize for his silence.

And someday, when she was ready, he'd tell her the rest. That she wasn't just part of his plans—she was the reason those plans mattered at all.

But not today. Today, friendship had to be enough. Today, understanding was what she needed.

And Riley Manchester was finally learning that sometimes, patience and love meant putting someone else's needs before your own desires.

Twenty-Two

RILEY

RILEY COULDN'T REMEMBER a drive into town ever dragging on like this one. Dust kicked up behind him, a gritty cloud that matched the restless energy in his mind. He gripped the steering wheel with his good hand, the radio playing softly, a background hum to his racing thoughts.

The guilt sat heavy in his chest. He should have reached out to her sooner, but each day of silence from her phone had hardened something in him. Pride, maybe. Or fear.

He'd checked his phone a hundred times, waiting for her name to light up the screen. When it hadn't, he'd told himself it was better this way—easier to focus on what the doctors were saying about his recovery, about whether he'd ride again.

Now he realized he'd been punishing them both with his silence, and for what? What exactly had he been trying to prove?

At long last, Bluestem came into view, the church spire standing tall against the morning sky. Riley's stomach tightened. He just needed to see her, to apologize for the silence, to let her know he was going to be fine. That was all. She'd driven to Sioux City after the accident, worried about him, and he owed her that much—a simple reassurance that he was okay.

The truck shuddered to a stop outside the Gazette. Riley took a deep, calming breath to steady himself, then pushed open the truck door and climbed out.

The bell above the Gazette's front door chimed as he stepped inside. Hannah looked up from her desk, her red hair piled haphazardly atop her head in what barely qualified as a bun. Her light floral perfume fought a losing battle against the distinctive scent of ink and paper.

"Riley!" Her face brightened as she dropped a stack of papers. "You're looking great! I always said one ornery bull could never keep Riley Manchester down for long.”

Her voice carried its usual cheer, but there was curiosity in her expression. She and Riley both knew this wasn't just a casual visit.

“Alyssa?” he asked, and the words came out shaky, even to his own ears. “Is she here?”

Hannah's expression shifted, her smile fading as if she'd been caught mid-laugh at a funeral. She hesitated for half a beat too long before answering.

“She's at the hotel,” Hannah said finally, her tone softer now, careful. “Packing.”

“Packing?” His voice came out rougher than he'd intended, and he cleared his throat. “Packing for what?”

“She's moving back to Chicago.” Hannah's eyes met his, full of apology. “I thought you knew.”

The words hit him like a second kick to the ribs. Packing. Chicago. Leaving. The simple apology he'd planned suddenly felt desperately inadequate. She was leaving—not just going back for a visit, but moving back. And he hadn't even had the chance to tell her he was okay, to explain why he'd been silent.

Something sharp twisted in his chest—fear, maybe, or the sting of regret for not getting here sooner. He turned away, running his uninjured hand across the back of neck.

"Riley?" Hannah's voice jolted him back to reality. "You all right?"

He wasn't. Not even close. But he wouldn't say that out loud. Not yet. Instead, he made a noise that wasn't quite a yes or a no and turned toward the door. His heartbeat drummed in his ears like horse hooves on concrete, relentless and loud.

"Did she say when?" The words were out before he could stop himself.

Hannah shrugged one shoulder—the kind of gesture that wasn't dismissive so much as resigned. "Soon. Maybe today."

He shook his head, trying to clear his thoughts. He couldn't let her leave without at least saying goodbye, without apologizing for his silence, without making sure she knew he was going to be fine. She deserved that much. Even if she'd already decided about Chicago, even if there was nothing he could say to change her mind, he couldn't let her go without seeing her one more time.

"I have to go," he said. "I have to talk to her."

Hannah rounded the corner of her desk and gave him a gentle push toward the door. "Then don't just stand there, Cowboy. Go."

Her words spurred Riley into action. He turned on his heel, nearly stumbling in his haste to get to the Whitemore. He wouldn't try to stop her from going back to Chicago. Not if her head and heart were set on that.

But at least she'd know he'd cared enough to come find her, to make sure she knew he was okay. At least he'd have the chance to say goodbye.

Twenty-Three

ALYSSA

Alyssa's bags stood by the front door of the Whitemore Hotel—two suitcases and a camera bag. They looked small against the hotel's grand entryway, like three obedient children, waiting to be packed in the trunk of Maggie's car. Maggie and LeAnne would ship everything else to Chicago later.

The kitchen door creaked—that familiar sound she'd grown accustomed to over the past months—and LeAnne stepped into the parlor carrying a tray with coffee. Steam curled from the spout of the ceramic pot, filling the air with a rich, comforting scent. She poured a cup and handed it to Alyssa, who wrapped both hands around the warm mug.

"You're sure about this?" LeAnne asked, her eyes searching Alyssa's face. "You can change your mind, you know."

"I know," Alyssa said, her throat tightening. She breathed in the coffee's aroma, trying to memorize this moment—the faded carpet with its intricate pattern worn thin in places, the steady ticking of the grandfather clock that had kept time for generations, the morning light filtering through lace curtains, casting delicate shadows across the room.

Alyssa set down her mug and moved to the window, staring out at Main Street. The morning sun cast long shadows across the pavement, and she could see Mrs. Peterson in her garden, pruning her flowers.

Soon, Maggie would be here and they would leave. They would drive to Omaha and spend the weekend with her folks. Then Maggie would return to Bluestem, and Alyssa would catch the Sunday flight to Chicago. By Sunday evening, she'd be back in her apartment, preparing for her first day back at the magazine. Back to deadlines and traffic and takeout food eaten at her desk.

No more lunches at Daisy's or evenings at the Rusty Spur. No more late nights at the

Gazette, arguing with Lenny over headlines and laughing with Hannah until their sides hurt. No more chance encounters with Riley.

Instead, she'd be back to the normal Chicago chaos she'd always planned to return to. So why did normal suddenly feel so wrong?

Because she was running. *Again*. She was running from Bluestem and the possibility of falling in love again, just like she'd run from Chicago and the reality of life there without Trevor.

"I need to finish packing a few things upstairs," Alyssa said. "I'll be right back."

LeAnne nodded, understanding in her eyes. "Take your time, Lyss."

Alyssa climbed the familiar stairs to her room, each step feeling heavier than the last. Inside, the space looked bare—most of her belongings already packed. Only three items remained on the dresser: the photo of her and Trevor in its silver frame, her broken camera, and the small velvet box meant to hold her engagement ring.

She picked up the photo first, tracing Trevor's smile with her fingertip. "I miss you," she whispered. "I miss you every day."

Her hand drifted to the chain around her neck, finding the engagement ring that rested against her heart. She'd worn it there for three years, unable to wear it on her finger but equally unable to tuck it away in its velvet box.

Now her fingers closed around it, the metal warm from her skin, and she let herself remember—really remember—for the first time in months. Trevor's laugh. The way he'd looked at her the day he'd asked her to marry him. The dreams they'd shared.

And then she thought about what Trevor would say if he could see her now, packed and ready to flee from the best thing that had happened to her in three years.

He'd tell her she was being an idiot.

The thought made her chest ache, but this time it wasn't the crushing weight of grief—it was something lighter. Something that almost made her smile.

Trevor had loved her. He'd wanted her to be happy. And she'd spent three years believing that happiness died with him in that hospital room. But what if it hadn't? What if it had just been waiting, hidden beneath her fear, until she was ready to reach for it again?

Running away from the possibility of love wasn't the answer—and it wasn't the way Trevor would have wanted her to live the rest of her life.

She thought about Riley: his patient smile, the way he'd never pushed her, never demanded more than she could give.

She wasn't ready to say she was in love with Riley. Her heart wasn't ready for that.

But it was ready to entertain the idea of staying in Bluestem a little longer. To see where things might lead with Riley—not rushing toward anything, not making promises she wasn't ready to keep, but simply... staying open. Staying present. Staying here.

She opened the door and started down the stairs, already forming the words she'd say to LeAnne. To Maggie. To Riley.

But as she reached the landing, she glanced out the window and her breath caught. Riley's pickup truck was pulling up in front of the hotel.

From her spot by the window, Alyssa watched as Riley climbed down from the truck. Even injured, with his arm cradled in a sling, he moved with quiet determination. She noticed the shadows under his eyes, evidence of sleepless nights, and the careful way he held himself to minimize the pain.

Alyssa's heart hammered against her ribs as she watched him carefully navigate each step. What was the man thinking? He could barely walk, let alone climb stairs.

Racing down the steps, she flung open the front door and rushed outside. "Riley, what are you doing?" she asked, reaching out to steady him as he faltered on the top step.

He attempted a smile, but pain flickered across his face. "Hey," he said, his breath coming in short bursts.

"Are you trying to break your other arm?" She guided him to the wicker loveseat and helped him to sit down, her hands gentle but firm on his good arm.

Riley shook his head. "I'm fine," he said, but relief washed over his face when he settled against the cushions. "I heard you were moving back to Chicago."

Alyssa blinked back tears. "You shouldn't have come, Riley. You shouldn't even be out of bed!"

The exhaustion on his face was clear, but so

was the determination. "A little pain won't kill me," he said. "But your leaving might."

The morning breeze ruffled his sandy hair. Without his usual cowboy hat, he looked younger somehow, less the confident rodeo cowboy and more the man who had held her in his arms and taught her how to two-step, who had made her laugh when she thought she'd forgotten how, who had looked at her in a way that made her feel truly alive again.

"I wanted to visit—" Alyssa began.

"I should have called—" Riley said at the same time.

They stopped, and Riley's lips curved slightly despite the tension. "You first," he offered.

Alyssa took a deep breath, the fresh morning air mixing with Riley's familiar aftershave. "I wanted to visit you at the hospital again, but after that first day, I just..." She trailed off, uncertain how to explain without revealing too much of her heart.

"I kept hoping you'd come back," Riley said, his voice quiet but steady.

"I couldn't," she whispered, the words catching in her throat. "Seeing you lying in that hospital bed, so still... it brought everything back." A single tear escaped and traced a path down her cheek.

Riley's expression softened with understanding, but he remained silent, letting her speak.

"After Trevor died, I promised myself I'd never be that vulnerable again. I'd never let myself need someone so much that losing them would..." She swallowed hard. "When you got hurt, all I could think was: Not again. I can't do this again."

Riley didn't interrupt, didn't reassure her with empty platitudes. He simply listened, his eyes never leaving hers, giving her the space she needed to say what she needed to say.

"I was so scared. It was easier to focus on going back to Chicago, back to my old life, than to face the possibility of—" Her voice broke, and she took a steadying breath. "Of letting someone in again. Especially someone who climbs on the back of a two-thousand-pound bull just for fun."

Riley's mouth turned up in a smile at her attempt at humor, but his eyes remained serious. He reached for her hand, his calloused fingers warm against hers.

"I understand fear, Alyssa," he said. "Every time I sit on a bull, there's that moment in the chute when everything goes quiet, and I think about all the ways it could go wrong. All the injuries I've seen, the close calls. That fear never really goes away." He gave her hand a gentle squeeze. "But then the gate opens, and I have to decide—do I let the fear win, or do I take the ride anyway?"

Alyssa looked down at their joined hands. "That isn't the same," she said.

"Isn't it?" Riley's voice was soft but insistent. "Opening up your heart. Letting someone in. That's the biggest risk there is. No safety equipment, no rodeo clowns to distract the danger, just... faith. Faith that it's worth it, even with the risk."

"I don't know if I'm brave enough," she said, her voice barely above a whisper.

"You're the bravest person I know," Riley said. "You came to a town where you didn't know anyone, threw yourself into stories that mattered, made friends, built a life. That takes courage, Alyssa. Real courage."

"That's different than—"

"Than learning to love again? Maybe. But I

think you're braver than you give yourself credit for."

Alyssa met his gaze, seeing nothing but sincerity there. "I don't understand. Why me?" she asked. "You could have anyone in Bluestem. Anyone."

Riley's smile widened, lighting up his entire face. "Do you think I haven't asked myself that a hundred times? Why you, a city girl, strolling into our town with your designer handbag, your high heels, and your remarkable skill for falling at my feet at the most inopportune moments?"

Alyssa blushed. "This from the man who just collapsed on the porch in front of me!"

Riley laughed, then winced. "Fair enough," he said. His voice softened. "But then I saw how you listened to people, really listened when they told you their stories. How you get this little crease between your eyebrows when you're concentrating on taking the perfect shot. How you reach for Trevor's ring when you're worried or thinking hard about something."

Alyssa's hand flew to the chain around her neck. She hadn't realized how obvious the gesture was.

"I don't want to replace him," Riley said, his

thumb tracing small circles on her wrist. "I'm just asking for a chance. A chance to see if what I feel for you—what I think you feel for me—is real."

Alyssa remained motionless, the warmth of his thumb on her wrist sending a tingling sensation up her arm. The subtle scent of his after-shave danced around her, stirring emotions she'd fought hard to keep at bay.

She thought back to her time in Bluestem—to the quiet evenings spent with LeAnne on this very porch, to the colorful characters she'd met because of the stories she'd written, to the memory of Riley's voice mingled with hers as they sang their hearts out heading to the rodeo in Scottsbluff. She thought of the woman she'd been when she arrived and the woman she'd become.

"What about Chicago?" she asked, though the question felt less urgent now. "My job, my apartment. My life is there."

Riley nodded. "I know. And I'm not asking you to give that up."

"Then what are you asking?" The question came out more vulnerable than she'd intended.

Riley's good hand moved to her face, his

touch feather-light. "I'm asking for time. Time to see if what we feel for each other is strong enough to build a future on."

His words echoed the conclusion she'd reached upstairs, and suddenly the decision felt clear. She'd already chosen, really, the moment she'd stood up from that bed and made the choice to stop running.

"What if we try and it doesn't work?" she asked, voicing her deepest fear. "What if I stay, and then something happens to you, or you realize I'm not what you want?"

"What if it does work?" Riley countered gently. "What if we take this chance and discover something amazing?"

The last piece of Alyssa's armor crumbled away. She reached out, allowing her fingers to trace the line of his jaw, the curve of his mouth.

For the length of an eight-second ride, he sat perfectly still, letting her explore. Then slowly, he leaned in, capturing her lips with his. The kiss was gentle and questioning, full of all the things they were afraid to say aloud. He pulled back first, his breathing uneven, and pressed his lips to her forehead.

"So," she said, her voice steadier than she expected, "how long would you like me to stay?"

Riley chuckled softly, a hint of relief in his voice. "Forever would be nice. But I'll settle for the rest of the summer."

Alyssa's eyes glistened with tears as she took a deep breath, the weight of her decision sinking in. "I think I can manage that."

The front door creaked open behind them. Alyssa turned to see LeAnne trying—and failing—to look innocent.

"Sorry to interrupt," she said, not looking sorry at all, "but Maggie's on the phone. She's wondering if you still need that lift to Omaha tonight."

Alyssa looked at Riley, then back at LeAnne. "No," she said, feeling happier than she had in three years. "You can tell Maggie there's been a change of plans. By the way, is my room still available for a few more weeks?"

LeAnne's face broke into a delighted smile. "Lyss, that room is yours for as long as you want it."

As LeAnne disappeared into the hotel, Riley wrapped his good arm around Alyssa's shoulders, pulling her close. "Hello, City Girl. Welcome to Bluestem."

"Why, thank you, Country Boy," Alyssa said, leaning into his warmth. "It looks like a wonderful place to visit."

Riley tilted his head slightly, brushing a light kiss against her temple. "Oh, it is. And it's an even better place to call home."

Alyssa nestled against him, embracing the comfort of his touch. "We'll see, Cowboy. We'll see."

Epilogue

ALYSSA

ONE YEAR Later

The late afternoon sun hovered over the horizon, painting the rolling hills of the Manchester ranch in soft gold. Alyssa and Riley walked hand in hand, the Niobrara River winding below them like a silver ribbon. The steady murmur of water over rocks drifted upward, mingling with the rustling of the tall prairie grasses and the occasional call of a meadowlark.

Alyssa closed her eyes and breathed in the sweet scent of alfalfa carried on the warm breeze. She opened them to find Riley watching her, his sandy hair catching the golden light, a smile playing at the corners of his mouth. One year ago, she had nearly left Bluestem, nearly left him. Now, walking next to him with their fingers intertwined, she could hardly remember why.

"Penny for your thoughts?" Riley asked, his thumb tracing small circles on her palm.

"I'm just thinking how different everything is from when I first came to Bluestem. I remember telling my boss I'd be gone three months, max."

Riley's eyes crinkled at the corners as his smile widened. "Now look at you. Maggie's right hand woman, freelancer for the Nebraska Life Magazine, and the only person in town who can make Hannah speechless."

"That happened once," Alyssa said, laughing. "And only because I told her I had permission from Maggie to print the picture of the mayor, sleeping, at the town council meeting."

Below them, cattle grazed in the distance, their occasional lowing carried up the hill by the gentle breeze. Wildflowers dotted the grassy slope in splashes of purple and yellow, their fragrances mingling with the scent of the river and sun-warmed grass. A hawk circled lazily overhead, looking for its next meal. Alyssa raised her camera and snapped a quick shot of the hawk against the blue Nebraska sky.

The past year had transformed them both. Alyssa had watched Riley shift from a man divided between family obligations and personal dreams to someone who had found his own path. The rodeo school had just been an idea then, a fleeting thought during his recovery. Now, it was taking shape below them, the renovated barn visible from their hilltop vantage point.

"Maggie asked about your dad today. She wondered how retirement's going for him." Alyssa brushed a stray wisp of hair back behind her ear as the breeze played with the loose strands. "I've been wondering that, too. How do you think he's adjusting?"

Riley laughed. "I think he's finally getting used to it." He paused, his voice softening. "He even admitted that Kate has the company running smoother than he ever did."

"And Kate likes being the boss?"

"Are you kidding? She was born for it," Riley said with a grin. "She called last week to tell me about some new contract she landed. I could hear the excitement in her voice—the same way

I feel when I'm teaching a kid how to read a horse's body language. We are both finally exactly where we belong."

As the afternoon light faded, Alyssa studied Riley's face—the tiny crinkles at the corners of his eyes, the faint scar along his jaw from his bull riding accident, the relaxed set of his shoulders.

He caught her looking and winked, making her roll her eyes even as warmth spread through her chest.

"What about you?" Riley asked, his voice softening. "Any regrets about giving up your life in Chicago?"

Alyssa shook her head without hesitation. "Not a single one. That life feels like it belonged to someone else."

"And Stan's job offer?" Riley prompted. Her former boss still called occasionally, the latest offer coming just last month.

"No regrets there, either," she said. She looked out over the rolling hills, the distant cattle, the river catching the sunlight. "This is home now. My stories are here."

"Who would have thought that your tumble into the middle of my bull ride could lead us here?" Riley asked, his eyes dancing with mischief.

Alyssa groaned. "Are you ever going to let me forget that?"

"Not as long as I live," he said, smiling. "It's my favorite story to tell the new students: And that, kids, is exactly how not to enter a rodeo arena."

"You're terrible," she said, but she was laughing. The memory no longer carried the sting of embarrassment. Instead, it had become part of their shared history, a story they could laugh about together.

The sun was beginning its slow descent toward the horizon, casting long shadows across the hillside and bathing everything in a warm, golden glow. Below them, the sign for the Manchester Rodeo School caught the light, the fresh paint gleaming. RIDE SAFE, RIDE SMART, it read. Riley's motto, now emblazoned for all to see.

"It's getting dark," Alyssa said. "Ready to head back?"

"Not yet," Riley said. "There's something else I want to show you before the sun sets completely."

Alyssa nodded, sensing a slight shift in his energy—a nervous edge that hadn't been there before. "Lead the way, Cowboy."

The path curved around a stand of cottonwood trees, their leaves rustling softly in the evening breeze. As they rounded the bend, Alyssa stopped short, her free hand flying to her mouth.

In a small clearing overlooking the river, Riley had created a secluded oasis. A simple wooden bench faced the water, surrounded by dozens of tiny lights strung through the surrounding trees. They weren't yet glowing in the fading daylight, but would create a magical effect once darkness fell. On top of the bench sat a small wicker picnic basket, a bouquet of wildflowers tucked against its side.

"Riley," she breathed, unable to find more words.

He tugged her forward gently, his nervousness now visible in every line of his body. "Do you like it?"

"It's beautiful." She turned toward him, her heart beating faster. "What's the occasion?"

Instead of answering, he guided her to the bench and motioned for her to sit. He remained standing, pacing a few steps away, then back. The golden sunlight cast his shadow long across the ground as he ran a hand through his hair.

"Remember our first trip to Scottsbluff?" he asked suddenly.

Alyssa smiled. "How could I forget? We sang the entire way there."

"Badly," he added with a flash of his usual grin.

"Very badly," she agreed, feeling her tension ease slightly. "And we danced."

"And you kissed me outside your hotel room." His voice grew softer.

"And promptly ran away."

Riley laughed, some of his nervousness melting away. "Yes, you did. Left me standing there wondering what hit me."

The sun dipped even lower, and a peaceful quiet settled around them, broken only by the gentle rustling of leaves and the lapping of water against the rocks in the river.

Riley finally stopped pacing and stood directly before her, his expression shifting to one of determined calm. He reached for her hands, drawing her to her feet.

"This past year has been the best year of my

life," he said, his voice steady despite the nervous energy she could feel radiating from him. "When you agreed to stay, I told myself I'd be content with however much time you wanted to give me. A summer, a year…"

He paused, swallowing hard. "But I was lying to myself. I don't want just some of your time. I want all of it. Every day, every year, for as long as we have."

Alyssa felt her breath catch as Riley slowly, deliberately, lowered himself to one knee. The world seemed to narrow to just this moment, this man, his eyes reflecting the golden light of the setting sun.

"This spot," he said, glancing briefly around them, "is where my great-grandfather proposed to my great-grandmother almost a hundred years ago. Where my grandfather proposed to my grandmother. Where my father proposed to my mother." His voice grew husky with emotion.

"Carter proposed to his high school girlfriend here too, although that didn't work out so well." A wry smile tugged at the corner of his mouth. "She said yes, then changed her mind a week later. Decided Nashville was where she needed to be."

"Nashville? Are you telling me Carter proposed to Dani Whitemore?"

"He did. Because Manchester men have a tradition of bringing the women they love to this spot." He turned to her then, his eyes reflecting the last golden rays of sunlight. "Some with better results than others."

He reached into his pocket and pulled out a small velvet box. With slightly trembling fingers, he opened it to reveal a ring with a single diamond set in a delicate gold band.

"Alyssa Downing," he said, his voice thick with emotion, "will you marry me?"

Alyssa stood frozen, her heart thundering in her chest. For a brief, fleeting moment, Trevor's face flashed in her mind—not as a barrier or a ghost, but as a beloved memory, a chapter in her story that had led her to this time, this place. She had loved him deeply, truly. And now, impossibly, miraculously, she loved Riley just as deeply. Different loves, both real, both part of her journey.

"Yes," she whispered, then louder, "Yes!"

Relief and joy washed over Riley's face as he slipped the ring onto her finger. It fit perfectly, catching the last rays of the setting sun in a burst of light. He stood and pulled her into his arms, his lips finding hers in a kiss that felt like coming home and setting out on an adventure all at once.

When they finally broke apart, both breathless, Alyssa couldn't stop the laughter that bubbled up from deep within her. "I can't believe you pulled this off! I'm a reporter—I'm supposed to notice things!"

"I had help," Riley said, his arms still wrapped around her waist. "Carter set up the bench and the lights. Kate created the bouquet with flowers from her greenhouse. LeAnne packed our picnic lunch and Hannah chose the champagne.

"And Maggie?" Alyssa asked. "Was she in on this, too?"

"Where do you think I got your ring size?"

Alyssa glanced down at the diamond sparkling on her finger. "It's beautiful. Simple but... perfect."

Riley's hand came up to cup her cheek, his thumb brushing away a tear she hadn't realized had fallen. "Like you."

The words sent warmth spreading through her chest, up into her face. She wanted to deflect the compliment, make a joke, but the look in his eyes stopped her. He meant it. After a year, she was beginning to believe he always would.

"So what happens now?" she asked.

"Now? We celebrate with LeAnne's almond tarts and Hannah's champagne."

"Before facing the rest of the committee, you mean?" Alyssa smiled. "I'm guessing they are waiting for us somewhere?"

"The Whitemore," Riley said with a grin. "But we don't have to go right away." His eyes darkened as he pulled her closer. "I'd like to have you to myself for a little while longer."

Alyssa rested her head against his chest, listening to the steady beat of his heart. The ring on her finger felt strange, yet somehow completely right. Like this place. Like this man. Like the life they would build together.

"I love you, Riley Manchester," she whispered against his shirt.

His arms tightened around her. "And I love you, soon-to-be Mrs. Manchester."

She lifted her head, one eyebrow raised. "Bold of you to assume I'm taking your name, Country Boy."

"Manchester-Downing?" he suggested, his eyes dancing with amusement.

"We'll negotiate," she said, reaching up to trace the line of his jaw. "We have plenty of time."

He kissed her forehead, her nose, and finally her lips. "Come on, future Mrs. Manchester-Downing-or-whatever-we-decide. Let's go tell everyone our news."

Hand in hand, with the stars beginning to emerge overhead, they walked up the hill toward their future—together.

Continue your journey to Bluestem with …

WINNING HANNAH'S HEART

On New Year's Eve at the Rusty Spur, Hannah Mitchell makes a split-second decision — she kisses a handsome stranger under the mistletoe. It's the kind of bold, romantic move her friends would expect from her... and the kind of moment that should have ended with a laugh and a good story to tell.

Instead, that kiss sets into motion the most entertaining chain of events Bluestem has seen in years — and suddenly everyone has an opinion about Hannah's love life.

As Valentine's Day draws closer, Hannah must navigate friendly rivalry, community chaos, and the dizzying possibility that her heart might not be as undecided as she thought.

Even a few words make a big difference.

Join JoAnn's Dream Team at www.JoAnnCharles.com/free and be the first to know when one of her ebook novellas is free on Amazon!

JoAnn Charles writes clean, heartwarming romantic novels filled with small-town charm, hope, and happily-ever-afters. Her Bluestem cozy stories celebrate love, laughter, and the power of community, set in a place where everyone knows your name and second chances are always on the menu.

When she's not writing about love in Bluestem, JoAnn can be found enjoying coffee with friends, dreaming up her next story, or spending time with her family.

She also writes children's books under the pen name **N. L. Sharp**.